To Jyoti

with Love
&
Blessings

PENUMBRA

Ray Boudi
&
Ray da.

24th of August
2019.

Published by

FiNGERPRINT!

An imprint of Prakash Books India Pvt. Ltd.

113/A, Darya Ganj, New Delhi-110 002,
Tel: (011) 2324 7062 – 65, Fax: (011) 2324 6975
Email: info@prakashbooks.com/sales@prakashbooks.com

facebook www.facebook.com/fingerprintpublishing
twitter www.twitter.com/FingerprintP, www.fingerprintpublishing.com

ISBN: 978 81 7599 381 5

Processed & printed in India

PENUMBRA

BHASKAR CHATTOPADHYAY

FiNGERPRINT!

To my teachers

Epigraph

When the truth lies in the dark, it may be stumbled upon by a keen eye. When the truth lies in plain view, it can be seen by all. But beyond the light, yet before the dark, lies a liminal space, where the only purpose of truth is to mislead. This enigmatic region is known as the Penumbra.

CONTENTS

The Invite

Dear Mr. Ray,

I hope my letter finds you in good health. I've recently been made aware that you are the son of my late cousin. I remember her fondly from my childhood days, which I spent in India. She and I were very close. Like me, she had a keen interest in the art of the Renaissance period. She was also a Western classical music aficionado. Perhaps due to our common interests, or perhaps due to her simple and kind nature, we became good friends.

I have grown quite old now. I have travelled around the world in the pursuit of art. Being an artist myself, I have not been able to ignore the call of an interesting subject, however remote the location of the subject may have been. My travels have made me lose touch with most of my kin. I now live in a secluded bungalow in the suburbs of your city. The coming Saturday, 11 January , happens to be my 60th birthday. I have invited a few friends and acquaintances to come and *spend the weekend with me. I would be delighted if I could count on your presence too.*

Suhasini was more than a cousin to me—she was my best friend. If you will consider this request of an old man and pay a visit to your uncle on his birthday, I would be greatly obliged. You'll find my address on the envelope.

Yours truly,
Rajendra Mukherjee

I received the letter by mail one particularly chilly and gloomy January morning. The sender's address was of a village hundred kilometres southwest of Kolkata. Of late, the skies had been overcast and a cold wave seemed to be passing through the city. There were talks about that winter being the harshest in the history of Kolkata. A depression had been reported over the Bay of Bengal, and a thunderstorm had been forecasted as well. Shops were opening late and closing early. Attendances in schools and offices were low. Trams and buses were running empty. Streetlamps were burning in the middle of the day, thanks to very little daylight. It seemed a sort of melancholy had descended upon the city, almost like a shroud of mist. It didn't seem wise to step out. I had borrowed an interesting novel from the library and planned to stay in bed with it over the weekend.

I would have been happy to throw the letter in the bin, had it not contained those few words about my mother.

My mother, you see, has always been a mystery to me. I have only seen her in photographs. I am told she died while giving birth to me. People in my family say that she was a beautiful and kind woman. My father—who died of a weak heart three years ago, a few days after my twenty-first birthday—used to tell me stories about my mother: how they met, how they became friends, how she helped him get over his smoking, and how she always wanted to raise a child. He used to tell me there was not a single person who would speak ill of her. She was an ever-smiling, ever-caring, soft-spoken, and gentle-natured friend to everyone.

As I was growing up, I gradually learnt that there were complications during my mother's delivery, and that she gave up her life in a bid to save mine. Somehow, perhaps in my subconscious, this created a sense of guilt in me. I felt helpless, and in my desperation to do something, I tried to learn as much about my mother as possible. Good thing was I had all the time to do so, because I myself had very few friends. My afternoons, in particular, used to be very lonely. I would often hunt around the house, exploring nooks and corners of old store rooms, rummaging through creaky ancient cupboards and rusty trunks for things that belonged to my mother—her pen, an old magazine, a faded postcard, a thimble, a magnifying glass, an old book with a flower crushed between its pages, and other such seemingly unimportant things. Things which were of immense value to me, because they helped me paint a picture of the woman I had never seen.

My own life had been pretty 'ordinary' and devoid of any interesting events. I grew up in Ranchi; my father was a doctor there. He was a man of impeccable values and principles. Stories are told about how he had responded to calls from patients within hours after my mother had passed away. Even with my limited knowledge of worldly matters as a child, I could sense that people in town had the highest amount of respect for him. He was a reticent man and although my relationship with him was distant, he was very fond of me. He had always been a workaholic, but people around me told me that after my mother's death, he had absolutely submerged himself in work. I hardly saw him all day. But I have faint memories of waking up in the middle of the night to find him sitting on my bed beside me, silently staring at me with tears in his eyes.

After my graduation, I came to Kolkata and began working as a freelance journalist. I would cover press meets, political rallies, inauguration events, things of such sort. I hadn't married and had no intention to. I was new to the city and had a tough time adjusting to it. I didn't have any friends here. One morning, as I had just come out of a shower, I received a call from my aunt in Ranchi, saying that my father had passed away. Although my father had hardly spent any time with me while I was growing up, after his death, for some strange reason, I became even lonelier. At times I felt like giving everything up and returning to Ranchi, only to remember that I hardly had any friends there as well. I was, as I mentioned earlier, not very social. In fact, I was quite shy and found it difficult to strike up a conversation. Not a very encouraging quality to possess for a journalist. Which is also why I seldom worked, and my finances were in bad shape.

Thankfully, my father had bequeathed a couple of properties in the city of Kolkata and the collective rent that I earned from them was more than enough for me to lead my simple life. I lived with a servant-cum-cook. He had been with us from our Ranchi days and he took care of me. I had no savings, nor did I have what people who follow the established patterns of a normal life would call a 'future'. I was simply walking through my life, and my life didn't seem to be going anywhere. But I didn't care. Because even if I would care, there seemed to be very little I could do about it, really. So, I ate well, watched at least one movie in the theatres in a week, kept myself immersed in books, and led a pretty uneventful life. And then the letter arrived.

It was a simple letter, with a simple message, but it managed to disturb the tranquillity of my ordinary existence. Here was a mysterious man, a man I didn't know, or one I had never even heard of, inviting me to a self-admittedly secluded bungalow in a remote village to spend a weekend with him on his birthday. What if it was some kind of a trap? These days one could never be too careful in such matters. On the other hand, he seemed to know so much about my mother, things that I myself didn't. Then again, therein lay another possibility— what if the information the gentleman was projecting wasn't true? I had no means of verifying if what he was claiming were facts.

I read the letter several times. The handwriting didn't seem to be like that of a sixty-year-old. Or perhaps the sender had had the letter written by someone else. Most interestingly, I had learnt for the first time that my mother had an interest in Renaissance art and Western classical music. I had heard that she had a good singing voice, but this revelation was news to me. I felt a sudden need to go, principally with the hope that the old gentleman would perhaps have a few photographs or letters of my mother. The strange urge that overpowered me can only be understood by someone who has never seen his or her parent. At the same time, I was scared at the prospect of the whole affair being a plan to put me in some kind of trouble. I was in two minds, and the dilemma kept me awake through the night.

On the morning of Saturday, 11 January, a realization dawned on me. What did a young, penniless man like me have to lose? Why would someone want to harm me? I hardly had any friends, let alone enemies. Most importantly, I had very little money. Also, what if this man was, in fact, who he claimed to be? What if he actually knew my mother and would be able to tell me more about her? The more I thought about it, the more I inclined towards accepting the invite. Finally, I made up my mind. I went to a nearby bookstore and bought a book on Art, got it gift-wrapped, came home, threw a few clothes and essentials into a rucksack, and started off in pursuit of a chance encounter with my mother's memories.

In the Middle
of Nowhere

The address on the envelope said that Mr. Mukherjee's bungalow was in a small village called Sanatanpur, off National Highway 41. Distance-wise, it wasn't too far from where I lived, but the bus I had taken from the city had made it a point to make a stop at every single neighbourhood in the south of the city, picking up passengers and goods, and it wasn't until quarter past four that it dropped me on the highway and vanished around the bend of the asphalt road. The moment the bus disappeared from my sight, I realized how quiet the place was. Those living in the city usually have their ears permanently tuned to a steady chatter of traffic, trading, and other sounds, and when they are suddenly and unceremoniously dropped in a peaceful environment, such as the one I presently found myself in, they feel a strange discomfort at first. I felt it too.

Everywhere I looked, I spotted trees of various shapes and sizes. Around me were tall bamboo groves, swaying mildly in the chilly breeze. I loved greenery. During my growing up years in Ranchi, I used to spend a lot of time in what novelists and poets like to call 'the lap of nature'. But when I came to the city, like several other things, I was forced to give up this luxury too. Yes, there was a tiny park near my house in Kolkata, but it gave me more hurt than joy. Sitting in that cramped and dusty place, my mind would often go back to the days I used to spend in lying down on a verdant field, watching a line of ants take pieces of dry leaf to a hidden home. The park near my house looked so artificial and so crowded that I soon stopped going to it. Now, standing by the side of the highway, as I turned my head and looked around, I realized how much I had missed being amidst such surroundings. There was an Indian cuckoo calling from some hidden place, and I stood motionless for a long time to hear its sweet singing.

I looked around and spotted a shanty tea stall at a distance. It was a small shop, with a low thatch roof. It had a couple of benches placed outside. An old and rickety Hero bicycle was parked next to the benches, with a large can of milk hanging perilously from its carrier. There was nothing else to be seen all around. As the lanky bamboo trees rustled and creaked, a gust of wind blew in my direction and a cold shiver shook me to my bones and dragged me back to reality in a hurry. It would get dark soon. What godforsaken place had the wretched vehicle brought me to? I walked up to the tea stall and greeted the owner. He was a man in his late fifties, with a weathered face that peeped out at me from behind a monkey cap that had perhaps been mauve in colour several winters ago. He greeted me back with a gesture and looked at me inquisitively.

I enquired about the address, but much to my despair he couldn't tell me anything about it. I looked out at the sky once again and didn't like the looks of it one bit.

I was looking around helplessly and wondering what to do, when a frail old man sitting on one of the benches with a glass of tea next to him, looked up from the crossword puzzle in the *Statesman* and asked me if I was looking for Rajendra Mukherjee, the artist. Much relieved, I took a couple of steps towards him and said that I indeed was, and that it would be very kind of him to direct me to his bungalow. The old man obliged, and having secured the directions, and paying no heed to the warning that it was a long walk from here and that it would start raining very soon, I embarked on my hike.

There is something about the countryside that acts as a stimulant for those who live in the city. Everyone knows that. But what very few people seem to realize is that the best way to truly enjoy that stimulant is to experience the countryside on foot. As I manoeuvred the unpaved, meandering, and sometimes muddy path, I soaked in the sights and sounds around me and filled my lungs with fresh air. And it seemed all my weariness and lethargy were slowly falling off like dead skin and that I was getting revitalized all over. Here and there, hidden behind trees and shrubs, I could see huts and brick houses of what seemed to me was a village. This must be Sanatanpur, I thought. There were hens and goats roaming around freely in the courtyards of the houses, and the mooing of cows could be heard. One or two women looked at me suspiciously from behind their windows and thrust their children towards the interiors of the house. Countless trees doted the sides of the path; guava, jackfruit, mango, banyan, peepal, and papaya were the ones I could recognize. Thanks to the season there were no flowers to be seen, but the chirping of birds made up for the lack of bloom. It was strange, really. The birds were constantly chirping, but it didn't seem noisy or boring even for a moment. On the contrary, they seemed so soothing that at times, I couldn't help myself but halt on my march, just to devote my entire attention to the sweetness of the sounds. But a quick glance at the skies would make me resume my walk immediately. Dark clouds had started gathering overhead and were threatening to burst open any moment.

Soon I realized that I was leaving behind the huts and houses of the village. The old man at the tea stall had told me that this would be so. As per his directions, I still had to walk a couple more kilometres. I continued on my path. There were now no signs of habitation all around, only open fields that extended away from the elevated pathway and merged into the distant horizon on both sides. The chirrup of birds had been replaced by the chirping of crickets. After walking for some more time, I suddenly realized that there was no sound at all. I stopped walking to confirm my suspicion, and realized that I was correct. I looked back. There was no one, not even a dog to be seen on the path anymore. It seemed I was standing in some strange and uninhabited land that God had created and forgotten all about. I whipped out my cell phone from my pocket and as I had suspected, there was no signal. The clock on the phone showed 5:17 p.m. I figured I probably had less than half an hour of daylight left to find the bungalow.

My mind went back to the letter and I felt a trifle nervous. In the initial effort at breaking the inertia of my ordinary life, and fascinated by the romanticism of the very idea, I had embarked upon a mysterious journey, but ground realities were soon catching up with me. I realized I should have at least called

Mr. Mukherjee to take proper directions to his residence. But then I remembered that the letter never mentioned a number, which seemed very strange. Did he not have a telephone, at least? I began to curse my decision. The more I thought about it, the more I realized it was a bad one, taken from the safe confines of my warm dwelling, without having considered any of the numerous dark possibilities that lay in the pursuit of something whose existence I wasn't even sure of. I began to repent my decision and realized that I would probably have a very unexciting experience over the weekend. Unexciting—fine, I thought—just let it not turn out to be nasty.

A booming and menacing rumbling sound originated from the skies and no sooner had it faded out over the distant horizon than the first drop of rain fell on my face, and I realized I was in trouble. Deep trouble. The fancy foldable umbrella I had packed in my rucksack was a flimsy little thing—purchased in a city mall at a heavy discount. There was no way it was going to save me from the onslaught of a torrential thunderstorm, that too in the open countryside. I looked back once again, wondering if I should go back and seek shelter in the village or just continue to push forward and hope to reach the bungalow before the rain picked up. I had very little idea of how much distance I was yet to cover, principally because in enjoying my long-lost contact with nature, I had not bothered to keep a track of how much distance I had already covered. The number of drops was increasing as I stood there, thinking. A young boy on a bicycle came from the opposite direction and rushed past me, ringing away his vehicle's bell furiously and quite unnecessarily—for who else was there besides him and me? I waved at him and asked him to stop, but he didn't listen, thanks perhaps to the steady drizzle that had now started. He rushed past me, leaving me alone and helpless in the middle of nowhere. Making up my mind, I flung my umbrella open, zipped up my jacket, and marched ahead double quick on the path, hoping that it would take me to the bungalow before the storm made landfall.

The Mukherjee
Bungalow

By the time I reached Mr. Mukherjee's bungalow, it had started raining cats and dogs. A strong gale accompanied the heavy rain, making things more difficult. The bungalow itself was in the middle of nowhere. There wasn't, from what I could see, a single house or shop or anything else in the vicinity. Just peaceful and uninhabited countryside. But this didn't make the bungalow stick out like a sore thumb. Instead, it seemed like a dream house to me, for the building itself bore evidence of good taste. It was an ideal house for an idyllic location such as this. The compound was wicket-fenced and deciduous trees, the branches of which were now swaying violently in intoxicated helplessness, skirted the main bungalow. There was a small pond on one side of the compound and I thought I caught a partial glimpse of what seemed like a cowshed towards the backyard. And as I ran the homestretch, I observed from the corner of my eye that there were two cars parked within the compound under a garage shed.

I knocked heavily on the front door, and was greeted by a young gentleman. He seemed to be in his mid-twenties, had a good physique, was dressed in a light brown pullover and jeans, and had twinkling, intelligent eyes.

"Are you Mr . . .?" He had to raise his voice because of the storm.

"Prakash Ray. I'm . . . err . . ." I hesitated.

"Mr. Mukherjee's nephew, I know. Please come in. You can leave your umbrella in the stand over there."

I stepped into the house and was relieved to have found protection from the menace outside. The gentleman brought me a dry towel, which I put to use. Then, I looked around and was at once impressed by the neatness and precision with which the hall had been decorated. One could tell, without having any prior knowledge, that there was an artist's touch in the house. Beautiful paintings hung on the walls, the furniture bore evidence of classic and old-worldly taste, vases of terracotta were placed strategically around the room, and the chandelier was a grand affair, and well maintained at that.

"Mr. Mukherjee is in his bedroom upstairs, and will be here shortly. Can I get you some coffee?" asked the young man, as I seated myself on a chair.

"Yes, please. Thank you."

As he disappeared into the interiors of the house, I wondered what a strange man Mr. Mukherjee must be to live in this secluded place away from the city. I figured this environment was ideal for his work. Artists have been known to prefer to live amidst nature, after all. I once again turned my eyes towards the paintings. I didn't have much knowledge on the subject. I wouldn't be able to distinguish between periods, or be able to tell one artist's work from another. But the paintings and the ornate frames had an elegance which drew my admiration. One of the paintings especially caught my attention—it was a portrait of a lady. Not Indian, most probably British, I thought. The lady was dressed in royal attire and the way the artist had captured the little details and nuances, the play of light and shade on her face, the glitter of her jewels, the intricate designs of her gown, the mellow environment of the room in which she sat in a listless manner, everything bore evidence to the fact that the artist was a master of his or her art. The signature caught my eyes— 'RM', and I realized the artist was Mr. Mukherjee himself. I admired the portrait for some more time, and then turned my attention towards the rest of the room—which had objects of art and craft strewn all around.

I noticed several bookcases filled with books, and wanting to take a closer look, I walked up to one of them. Most of the books were on art. There were a few books on pottery and quite a few on music and history as well.

An old servant entered the room just then with a tray in his hands. Coffee and pastry were served. Soon after, the young man walked back into the room.

"You must be . . .?" I enquired.

"Oh, silly me! I should have . . . My name is Arun Mitra. I'm Mr. Mukherjee's secretary."

"Oh, I see."

Mr. Mitra came across as a smart and polite young man. There was an air of calm confidence around him.

"In fact, I was the one who wrote the letter to you," he

said. "I take dictations from Mr. Mukherjee because he can't write or paint anymore."

"I'm sorry to hear that," I said, wondering if I should ask why.

"Yes, he used to be a famous painter. In the eighties he was widely considered to be one of the most famous artists in Europe. He has written several books on art as well. A very learned man."

"When did he leave India?" I asked.

Arun Mitra gestured towards the table and said, "Come, your coffee's getting cold."

We settled down in our chairs and he continued: "As far as I know, he left India in the early seventies. He was in his teens then. His father was a renowned neurosurgeon in Kolkata, and didn't approve of his penchant for art. He ran away from home and went to Bombay. There, he worked as an apprentice for an artist named Campbell for a few months. This artist was a British national and was on a year-long painting tour through the subcontinent, particularly Sri Lanka and the Malabar Coast. After a few months, Campbell had to cut his trip short and leave for London. The artist had liked the fire in his young apprentice's belly, and decided to take young Rajendra Mukherjee along. Soon after reaching London, Campbell passed away in a car crash, and Rajendra Mukherjee was left to fend for himself. He neither had the money nor the wish to return to India. During the first few years, he drifted from one city to another, doing odd jobs like waiting at cafes, lifting crates, even working at a cemetery as a grave digger. Finally, he reached Rome and started sketching for a local magazine for a paltry sum. His sketches became famous and so did he. It was an upward journey from there, and he saw success very soon. He used to get calls from several prominent businessmen and aristocrats in different European cities, you know? Maharaja, that's what they called him. He came to be known as a famous portrait artist. But Mr. Mukherjee was not the kind of man to be satisfied with one genre of art. He soon shifted his attention to painting landscape. There too, his skill was proven beyond any doubt, and Mr. Mukherjee established himself as an undisputed expert in the field of painting in the whole of Europe."

Arun Mitra paused to catch his breath and I took another sip of my coffee. It was quite astonishing that such a famous and interesting man was living like a recluse in a small village in the suburbs of Kolkata.

"But, good times don't last long," he went on, "and Mr. Mukherjee was no exception to the rule. In Genoa, he met a count who had a fine stable of horses. He invited Mr. Mukherjee for a ride one day, and Mr. Mukherjee accepted. He shouldn't have. Because he had never ridden a horse before. The horse threw him off its back, and Mr. Mukherjee fractured his right thumb in the fall. The count was apologetic and spared no expense in his treatment, but the fracture was never perfectly mended. That was the end of Mr. Mukherjee's career as a painter. He did everything he could to check his downward slide, but fate had only so much to spare for him. He did, under those circumstances, what was perhaps the most intelligent thing to do. He began to write. His vast knowledge of art and first-hand experience helped him immensely, and he made the best use of them. He hired a secretary who would take dictations from him. Soon, the who's-who of European art circles realized that Mr. Mukherjee was as good a wordsmith as he was a painter. But deep in his heart, Mr. Mukherjee was an artist, and he was devastated by the fact that he would not be able to paint anymore. This began to tell upon his health too. After a few years, he decided to return to India."

A short gasp of exclamation escaped my lips. "That's some story!"

"Yes, a very interesting life indeed," said Arun Mitra with a smile.

"Have you been with him for some time?"

"Ever since he bought this house and started living here. Must have been, let's see, a few months shy of five years now?"

"Where are you from, originally?"

"I'm from Siliguri. After my schooling, I came to Kolkata. I studied in City College and was assisting a librarian friend of mine, when I was introduced to Mr. Mukherjee, who was looking for a secretary. He spoke to me for ten minutes, and offered me this job. I accepted, on the spot. He has a strong personality, you know? It's quite difficult to say 'no' to him. Moreover, I didn't have any reason to—the salary he offered was quite good, and I anyway wanted to live in the countryside. I have the bad habit of writing poetry, you see?"

Arun Mitra smiled amiably. The twinkle in his eye was unmistakably that of a bright and sincere young man. From his account of Mr. Mukherjee's life, it was obvious that he thought very highly of his employer and was completely dedicated to him.

"Oh, by the way," he said, "you won't get a cell phone reception here. So, if you need to make a phone call, you can use the telephone in the study."

"Yes, I was about to ask you that. I didn't realize that this place was so . . . err . . . cut off."

He smiled. "The population is quite low. The nearest town is more than forty kilometres away."

"Does Mr. Mukherjee live here all by himself?"

"No, there's his wife—his second wife. She is of an Indian origin, but she was born and brought up in London. Mr. Mukherjee has an apartment in the city and his wife keeps shuttling between the flat and this house from time to time. Other than Mr. and Mrs. Mukherjee and myself, there's also a servant—the one who brought you coffee."

"And Mr. Mukherjee's children?"

There was an unmistakable hesitation in Arun Mitra's response.

"Well . . . he has a son . . . from his first marriage. He returned to India with his mother soon after the accident in Genoa. I don't know if I should say this, but he was . . . you know . . . never too fond of his father, thanks to his single-minded devotion to art. I think he felt neglected. After coming to India, he and his mother stayed with her parents in Kolkata. After his mother's death, when Mr. Mukherjee didn't come to India to perform her last rites, the last iota of his love for his father vanished. And the final nail in the coffin was hammered in when Mr. Mukherjee married his second wife a few years later."

Arun Mitra paused briefly. He had a frown on his face, and his gaze was fixed at the floor. He said, almost in a murmur, "Sometimes, one does things which one later repents. I have heard Mr. Mukherjee say that he regretted the fact that he didn't come to India to support his son after his wife's death. Perhaps with old age, the father in him admonished the brash, erratic, and whimsical artist that he once used to be, and he was ready to make amends. But it was too late. His son didn't love him anymore. He had taken to drinking and gambling. When Mr. Mukherjee came back to India and bought this bungalow, he tried to persuade his son to come and stay with him, because he didn't have any children from his second marriage. He wanted to rehabilitate the only son he had. But he refused. The countryside didn't interest him. Now, he is too busy betting and losing money in the clubs of Kolkata. Moreover, he is not very comfortable around his stepmother. In fact . . . he . . . he simply can't stand the sight of her. He does come, once every month or so, usually when he is broke, and Mr. Mukherjee gives him money. But not without a showdown. His son leaves cussing and swearing, and Mr. Mukherjee is left all by himself, licking his own wounds."

I was noticing the young man closely as he spoke. There was deep sorrow in his voice. It was obvious, for he was close to the old man's grief. He could see it every day, and perhaps do nothing at all to allay his master's pain.

I waited, motionless. The atmosphere had become quite heavy. Dusk had already fallen, the weather had worsened outside and the room was getting darker by the minute. It was high time someone switched the lights on.

"Well," said Arun Mitra, coming suddenly back to the present with a cheerful smile on his face, "hopefully, the house will be lively over the weekend. We already have five guests amidst us, including you, and we are expecting two more guests to join us tonight."

"Oh, I didn't realise there were guests here already. I'm sure it'll be fun," I smiled.

"Ah, and here he comes," said Arun Mitra, as he rose from his chair and looked behind me. "Mr. Ray, allow me to introduce you to your uncle, Mr. Rajendra Mukherjee."

Rajendra Mukherjee

The servant had switched the lights on, illuminating the hall and revealing before me a tall, imposing figure, dressed in spotless white kurta pyjama. He looked quite young for his age. His hair, not all white, was drawn neatly towards the back of his head. He had a fair complexion, was clean-shaven, and had sharp facial features. He had a piercing gaze and presently, a soft welcoming smile lingered on his lips.

He didn't say a word for quite some time. He simply kept looking at me. I didn't know what to say either. After almost a minute, he gestured towards my chair.

"Sit, please." His voice matched his personality. I can't explain why but I suddenly began to feel a little nervous.

"I hope you didn't have much trouble looking for the house?" he asked in the same baritone voice.

"Not at all," I lied.

There's a perception in people's minds that an artist would have long flowing hair, nimble hands, and an extremely dreamy disposition. Mr. Mukherjee didn't seem to possess any such qualities. He seemed like a no-nonsense man who liked to deal with things in a matter-of-fact way. At the same time, he was far from being curt or impolite. On the contrary, his voice and manner of speaking were quite soothing. His eyes were fixed on me for some time; it seemed he was trying to read me like a book. The silence became quite uncomfortable, and I was almost about to say something, when the old man spoke softly.

"You have your mother's eyes."

I smiled shyly and shifted my gaze from him and looked at Arun Mitra. He was standing in one corner of the hall with his hands behind his back, waiting patiently and respectfully for his employer to continue the conversation.

"You have met Arun," continued Mr. Mukherjee. "There are a few guests here already. They must be in their rooms at present, but they will be joining us any moment now."

"I believe you are expecting a few more guests tonight?" I asked.

"Yes, I am."

I again sank into an uncomfortable silence, not knowing what to say. Mr. Mukherjee was still looking straight at me with his piercing gaze. A soft appreciative smile lingered on one corner of his lips. I suddenly dipped my hands into my rucksack, and walked up to the old man.

"I . . . umm . . . this is a small gift for you . . . err . . . happy birthday!"

Mr. Mukherjee's expression changed. He let out a hearty laughter which filled the entire hall.

"Thank you, sir!" he said with a mischievous smile. "Thank you, indeed. May I see what's inside?"

"Yes, please."

He carefully unwrapped the package in an orderly fashion and looked at the book inside. His eyes sparkled with appreciation and joy.

"Why, this seems to be an amazing book! I'm sure it'll be a good read."

"Well, I don't know much about the subject, but your letter said that you . . . so . . ."

"Thank you, I really appreciate your gift. I'm going to enjoy reading this."

I smiled. My nervousness was coming down. The man wasn't as intimidating as I had thought. The more I looked at him, the more I began to like him.

"Well, Mr. Ray—"

"Please call me Prakash."

Mr. Mukherjee smiled in approval.

"All right, Prakash. Tell me about yourself."

I hadn't expected the question, but I should have. It was obvious that it would come, but unprepared as I was, I had no idea where to begin. No one had asked me that question, not in years, at least. One of the facets of leading a life devoid of friends and acquaintances is that you don't have to, or get to, talk about yourself. I was completely stumped. Sensing my condition, perhaps, Mr. Mukherjee himself came to my rescue.

"What do you do for a living, if I may ask?" he said in a soft voice, trying to make me comfortable.

"I'm a freelance journalist."

"Oh! A noble profession. You're a truthmonger!" he

said with a smile, with an almost unnoticeable tinge of good-natured sarcasm in his tone, which I caught.

"And what do you like to do outside of work?" he asked.

"I am interested in films and sometimes I—"

"Films? You mean photography?"

"No, films as in pictures."

"Pictures?"

"Movies. Err . . . motion pictures."

"Oh, you mean the cinema?"

"Yes."

"I see. What else?"

"Most of all, I like reading."

"An admirable habit. What do you read?"

"Well, all kinds of subjects, but primarily fiction."

"Very good. I believe one can never be truly enlightened without reading. We don't exist in the times when one may hope to achieve enlightenment through meditation. Or, at least, I can't do so myself, and I don't know of anyone who has been able to. Do you?"

"I-I can't say I do."

"Hmmm."

I was badly in need of a glass of water, because my mouth was parched, although I realized I hadn't talked much at all, and had finished my coffee merely minutes ago. I forced a cough and turned towards Arun Mitra.

"If you don't mind, may I have a glass of water?"

"Sure," he said, "I'll have it sent for you. Would you care for another cup of coffee?"

"No, thank you."

"Arun," said Mr. Mukherjee, "would you also ask Mahadev

to set up the table for our guests? And see if Anita is ready to come down."

"Certainly, sir."

When Arun Mitra left, Mr. Mukherjee turned to me and said, "You must be wondering if I really am your uncle."

"What? No, not really. I-I . . ." I stammered.

"I think we can do something about that. Firstly, your mother's elder sister—your aunt Nilima, who gave me your address—she should be able to tell you about me if you ask her."

"There's no need, really." I felt quite embarrassed, even to think that back at home I had suspected the entire thing to be a sham.

Mr. Mukherjee smiled and went on. "And secondly, I have a letter. A letter that your mother wrote to me when she was expecting you. I intend to show it to you tomorrow."

My heart started beating faster, but I remained quiet. Outside, the storm lashed on. Mr. Mukherjee stood up.

"Your mother, Prakash, was a particularly kind-hearted woman. She was dreamy, and had a very positive and uncomplicated view of life. I was in Vienna when I received this letter. I used to write to her too. After all, she was the only one in my family who ever supported me. She was my friend. In the letter, Suhasini wrote about you. She said how happy she was to be expecting you and of all the wonderful plans she had for you. Raising you was all that she ever wanted to do."

I felt a choking sensation in my throat. I could feel better with that glass of water.

"I later learnt that she died in childbirth," he continued, "and I was devastated. I also learnt about your father from Nilima. I am so sorry."

I sat there in silence. The clock on the wall was ticking away. I felt a strange kind of emptiness within me. It was after a long time that someone had spoken to me about my parents. I missed them sorely and felt lonelier than ever.

Mr. Mukherjee turned to face me and looked straight at me.

"Prakash, I have invited you here because you are Suhasini's son, and because you are like a son to me. My own son—"

He didn't complete the sentence, because the servant had entered with the glass of water. Arun Mitra followed him into the hall.

"Sir, the guests have all gathered in the dining room. Tea has been served. Mrs. Mukherjee is at the table too," announced his secretary.

"We will be there in a few minutes," said Mr. Mukherjee. "Ask everyone to carry on."

"Very well, sir," said Arun Mitra and left the hall.

"As I was saying," Mr. Mukherjee continued, "my own son has led a . . . how shall I say . . . a wayward life, and I can't say I blame him for it. I myself have led an unrestrained and adventurous life till not very long ago. I was spirited, full of energy, hot-headed, and a brash and adventurous kind of man. But now I am old and exhausted. I have earned a lot but have lost much, much more. And standing at the far end of my life, I have realized that all that matters is the ties of blood. I wanted to meet you and I also wanted to ask you if you would agree to do a certain thing for me. You may consider this an old man's wish, or call it anything that you may please. But I'm sure you have the maturity and the intelligence to do this. Will you help me?"

I couldn't respond, for at that moment, there was a heavy knock on the door.

The Guests

"Would you open the door for me, please?" asked Mr. Mukherjee. I had still not been able to fully comprehend what he was talking to me about a few moments earlier, and had to wake myself out of a daze to rise and walk up to the door. As I opened the door, I realized it was quite windy outside and it was still pouring heavily. And in the middle of such ominous weather, my eyes caught the sight of a strange man. He was quite tall, and had a stocky build with very little neck. He was dressed in an old, shabby, and tight-fitting Duckback raincoat. He seemed to be in his mid-forties and had a head full of unkempt hair, which were now dripping with water. He was dancing around the veranda, struggling with an umbrella that had failed him and turned inside out, thanks to the strong winds. It was, as a matter of fact, a pretty comic sight to behold, and I was almost beginning to enjoy the situation, when the gentleman realized he had a spectator.

"Well, don't just keep standing there. Come and help me, for heaven's sake!" shouted the funny man.

I hopped onto the wet veranda and together we managed to rein in the unruly umbrella. It was quite evident that he would not be able to use it again.

"What a pity!" the gentleman said looking at the umbrella with grief all over his face. "Poor thing! Twenty years it was with me!"

"Aren't you going to come in?" I asked, as I myself didn't intend to stay outside in the biting cold and mourn the demise of his dear umbrella.

"Of course I'm going to step in, young man," he shouted over the howling of the wind and the clap of the thunder. "But who are you?"

"I'm Mr. Rajendra Mukherjee's nephew," I said—this time with confidence.

"Are you? Well, Mukherjee never said anything to me about a nephew. But why should I care, I'd rather stay inside with you, than outside with this blasted storm."

I showed the gentleman in and helped him take off his raincoat. Mr. Mukherjee greeted him warmly.

"Johnny!" Mr. Mukherjee let out an exclamation and embraced the funny man.

Johnny?! That's a strange name for someone from these parts of the country, I thought. Could be one of Mr. Mukherjee's friends from Europe. The inconvenience of travelling through the storm was clearly visible on his face, and he made no attempt to hide it.

"What a mess, Mukherjee! Don't tell me you were born on a night like this?" asked 'Johnny' with the mother of all grimaces on his face.

"Well, let me see," said Mr. Mukherjee, faking an expression of deep thought. "I can't seem to remember!"

Both laughed heartily, and Mr. Mukherjee turned to me.

"Prakash, meet Mr. Janardan Maity, my dear friend. Johnny, this is my nephew, Prakash Ray."

"We've met," said Mr. Maity, "under pretty rough circumstances. Don't you think, young man?"

"Made pleasant by your acquaintance, sir," I said with a polite smile.

Mr. Maity's eyes sparkled. "A smart young man! I like him, Mukherjee. He reminds me of my own golden days."

Mr. Mukherjee said, "Prakash, Johnny is a very special friend of mine, and I assure you that by tomorrow you'll see that you have won the friendship of a gentleman who has a golden heart."

"And a large appetite. I'm starving, Mukherjee. Where's the cake?" quipped Janardan Maity.

"Come, let's go into the dining room, all the other guests must be waiting for us," said Mr. Mukherjee, and we walked towards the interior of the house and stepped into the dining room.

The dining room too was as beautifully and artistically decorated as the main hall. In the centre of the room, there was an old-fashioned oval dining table, and presently, there were three ladies and three gentlemen, including Arun Mitra, seated around it, surrounding a beautiful birthday cake. Everyone rose on seeing Mr. Mukherjee enter, and to our surprise, one of the ladies, the youngest one, broke into a familiar song:

"Happy Birthday To You!
Happy Birthday To You!

Happy Birthday Dear Raja!
Happy Birthday To You!"

Everyone joined in with smiles on their faces. Mr. Mukherjee cut the cake and everyone clapped heartily. After the bantering and jokes that usually accompany such a ceremony, the servant took the cake into what seemed like an adjoining kitchen. Mr. Mukherjee requested everyone to take their seats and stood before his chair at the head of the table. I sat next to Arun Mitra. Mr. Mukherjee took a moment to choose his words, and began speaking in his baritone.

"My friends, my dear dear friends! What immense pleasure you have given this old man by accepting his invitation. As all of you would know, I turn sixty today. I woke up this morning and the first thing that came to my mind was—My word! Has it really been that long? I have, as you are aware, led a very colourful life, quite literally. My life was full of adventure, and I have seen, in my times, some of the most beautiful things God has created. I think I can say, without any hesitation whatsoever, that I have lived my life to the full."

Mr. Mukherjee paused. I threw a quick glance around the table. Everyone's eyes were fixed on the host, and everyone seemed to have great respect for him.

"I am happy to see, gathered in this room today, the people who are dearest to me. To tell you the truth, this birthday party is nothing but an excuse. What matters to me the most is that over the next few hours I'll have the pleasure of your company, and the pleasure of introducing you to each other. I hope, no, hope is not the right word, I'm certain that all of you will find new friends in this house over tonight and tomorrow. And that will be the greatest gift that this old man can receive on his birthday."

Everyone applauded to shouts of 'Hear, hear'. I had already begun to like my uncle. He went on:

"Some of you know each other, some of you don't. So, I am now going to do a formal round of introductions around the table. Of course, this is just to get your conversations started."

He paused again to let the sound of a loud thunderclap fade out. Tea, cake, and snacks were being served around the table by the servant. Mr. Mukherjee gestured to the lady on his left and said, "My wife, Anita. She hardly needs any introduction, as she is known to almost all of you. Anita and I met in London. A friend of mine had taken me to see a staging of *Othello*. I was mesmerized by Anita's performance as Desdemona. She was extremely talented."

My aunt had a sweet and calm face, and came across as a smart and intelligent lady with a genial nature. She would have been in her mid-forties. She smiled warmly and remarked with a slight accent, "No amount of flattery will get you a slice of that cake, Raja."

Everyone laughed, and Mr. Mukherjee shrugged his shoulders and winked at us mischievously. "No, jokes apart, I really mean it. She was good; she was very good. A common friend introduced me to her after the show and soon, we fell in love. She came into my life at a time when I was going through a dark phase. After Aparna passed away, I . . . I was . . ." Mr. Mukherjee seemed to choke. His face looked quite pale, although he forced the smile to stay on.

"Oh, come now . . ." said Mrs. Mukherjee as she held her husband's hand firmly, and smiled politely at us.

Mr. Mukherjee seemed to regain his composure and patted lovingly on his wife's supportive hand. He seemed a little embarrassed.

"I'm sorry. I'm sorry . . . Where were we? Ah yes, seated next to my wife is my trusted friend and legal advisor, Mr. Animesh Sen. I met Animesh's father in London. He was studying law when I was looking for work. We were roughly of the same age, and seeing a countryman in distress, he gave me shelter, for which I have been and will always be indebted to him. After completing his studies, he returned to India and set up a law firm in Kolkata. We stayed in touch for some time but then lost contact for many years. When I returned to India five years ago, I looked him up and we ended up becoming close friends. But he passed away around two years ago, and after his death, Animesh has taken over my legal affairs. Animesh is a great bridge player, I must tell you." Mr. Mukherjee smiled, and Animesh Sen nodded greetings to everyone around the table.

I observed him closely. He was in his early thirties and had sharp features. His sharp and always-wary disposition was quite lawyer-like, but he seemed very restless. He was constantly doing something or the other—either passing the plate of cookies across the table, or dusting off a few grains of sugar from the tabletop. I noticed he avoided making eye contact with anyone and gave the distinct impression of someone trying to hide something.

"Seated to Animesh's left is Mrs. Nandita Chaudhuri. Mrs. Chaudhuri and her husband used to own this house earlier. Unfortunately, he passed away at roughly the same time when I returned to India and I bought it from her because she wanted to move to the city with her daughter. Mrs. Chaudhuri now stays in North Kolkata. She sometimes graces this house with her presence. Her knowledge of roses is practically legendary. My servant Mahadev used to be at her service previously, and even now both of them take extremely good care of the garden. This house wouldn't be half as beautiful had it not been for her magic touch."

"I couldn't agree more," said Mrs. Mukherjee and smiled at Mrs. Nandita Chaudhuri.

I looked at Mrs. Chaudhuri with admiration and respect. There was something in her personality which led me to believe she was an honest and upright woman. She was short and thin, maybe in late forties or early fifties, but she held her head high and had a motherly aura about her. She seemed like this intelligent problem-solver whom everyone could trust. At the end of Mr. Mukherjee's introduction of her, she didn't smile or say anything. She just tilted her head slightly on one side and waited for him to carry on with the next introduction.

"The next person I'd like to introduce is a darling friend of mine. She is also like a daughter to me. Preeti studies Art at the Government College in the city. One of her professors told her about me, and ever since she has been hounding and pestering me with a series of interviews."

"I'm writing a biography on uncle's amazing life," the girl said, "right from his teenage days when he fell in love with Masaccio and Mantegna, to his stellar rise in the art circles of Europe, and up to his return home."

"That's right," smiled Mr. Mukherjee. "I have had to submit myself to her authority and interrogation, and I am eagerly awaiting the completion of her book, mainly because it will mean the end of her long interview sessions with me."

Preeti laughed heartily. She was roughly my age, perhaps a few years younger. She was smartly dressed, was quite attractive, and had a very comely and ever-smiling face. Although she was my age, it seemed to me that there was little else that was similar between us. She came across to me as very smart and confident in her communication. I also noticed that Mrs. Mukherjee's expressions had changed when her husband was introducing Preeti. The smile still lingered, but, somehow, it didn't feel genuine.

I was watching Preeti, when I suddenly noticed that Mr. Mukherjee was staring at the empty chair between Preeti and myself with a blank expression. After a few moments, he spoke.

"Some of you have met Narendra, my son. I was hoping to have him here with us tonight, but it seems he must have been caught up with something."

There was a clear sense of discomfort felt around the table. Arun Mitra hung his head and fiddled with his palm, Animesh Sen rubbed his nose with his knuckle and Janardan Maity cleared his throat. Mrs. Chaudhuri's expressions didn't change and Preeti shifted in her chair. I felt the discomfort too, and didn't know what to do when Mr. Mukherjee, led by a soothing gesture from his wife, decided to break the silence and went on.

"Anyway, we were talking about those who are here with us today, not about those who aren't. Next, allow me to introduce to you a fine young man—my nephew Prakash Ray. He is a journalist and he lives in the city. His mother and I were cousins and best friends during our childhood. She was a gem of a person. Although I've never met her husband—Prakash's father—but I have been told that he was an extremely well-respected and upright gentleman as well, and it all shows in Prakash. You'll find him possessing an amiable and gentle manner and it'll take you merely minutes to befriend him."

Janardan Maity raised his hand and said, "I can vouch

for that. Mr. Ray and I became friends over an umbrella fight earlier this evening."

Everyone laughed, including me.

"All of you know Arun," Mr. Mukherjee continued. "Arun is, quite frankly, my life support system. I don't know what I would do without him. He manages my life for me. He is extremely intelligent, remarkably efficient, and a very sincere and promising young man."

Arun Mitra spared a shy smile and simply said, "Mr. Mukherjee is too kind."

"The next person I would like to introduce to you is my younger brother— Devendra. I myself hardly get to meet him; he being a doctor in the city and a very busy man. He is a thorough professional and will only accept my invitations if there's a medical need. Sometimes, I have even had to fake a fever or a bellyache to drag him down here. Isn't that right, Dev?"

Devendra Mukherjee seemed like a no-nonsense guy. He was smart, handsome, and had a strong built. He rubbed the brown skin off a few roasted peanuts, put the white nuts in his mouth, and remarked, "Your heart is beginning to worry me, you know?"

"Damn my heart!" smiled Mr. Mukherjee. "I'll live as long as I want to. In fact, all of you should know that this pesky rascal and I have always been polar opposites in our interests as well. As a child, I used to paint and read, and Dev was into football. He was quite good at it, actually. Centre-forward, right?"

The last question was directed at Devendra Mukherjee, who took a sip from his cup and remarked, "That was a long time ago."

"And finally, we come to my dear friend Janardan Maity," said Mr. Mukherjee. I was afraid Janardan Maity would actually interrupt him and do his introduction himself, but I saw that he allowed his friend to speak.

"Johnny, as I like to call him, is an interesting character. There are very few things that he is not interested in, but as he himself admits, he doesn't excel in doing anything at all. I met Johnny at the National Library, and we soon became good friends. He is my chess partner, and despite a huge age difference, we don't miss a chance to pull each other's legs. Johnny's ancestors used to be zamindars in what is now known as Bangladesh, and don't let his austere disposition fool you— he is quite well off. He doesn't stick to a regular job, and does whatever he likes. He is a voracious reader and has a good sense of humour, and my lonely days become so much livelier when he is around."

Janardan Maity looked around the room and smiled politely.

"Oh, and one more thing," said Mr. Mukherjee, looking straight at Janardan Maity with a strange spark in his eyes, "In the last five years that I have known him, I have never won a game of chess with Johnny, and I can assure you that I am myself quite good at the game. I've vowed to checkmate him some day."

"Hah! That'll be the day, Mukherjee!" said Janardan Maity, waving dismissively.

"Well, that's all folks," rounded up Mr. Mukherjee with a cheerful smile. "That's all I had. Please enjoy yourselves."

The Man
in the Rain

After tea, we returned to the main hall, and soon conversations started in isolated groups. Left all alone by myself, I spotted Animesh Sen standing by the bookcase, speaking to Janardan Maity, who was listening to him attentively. I turned towards the other side of the room to find Preeti having an animated conversation with Arun Mitra. It was nice to see that the party was warming up, but at the same time, I was feeling a little odd standing there all by myself. I was just beginning to wonder where Mr. Mukherjee was when I noticed Nandita Chaudhuri walking up to me.

"Pretty rough weather," she said in a conversational manner.

"Yes, I had stepped out sometime back, and it's raining cats and dogs."

"Mr. Mukherjee has nice things to say about you."

"Well," I smiled and said, "we've just met, less than an hour ago."

"Some people have the ability to create a very good first impression."

I smiled shyly. Then I said, "I can't see Mr. Mukherjee around."

"He has gone to his room for some time. I was speaking to him a few minutes ago."

"You stay in North Kolkata?"

"Yes. Bagbazar."

"I see."

"Where do you stay?"

"South. Ballygunge."

"Ah!"

I looked around the hall and remarked, "I have to say that this is a beautiful house. I haven't seen it all, but whatever little I did see, I can only admire it."

"Well, thank you!" said Mrs. Chaudhuri, and immediately her face was shrouded with an unmistakable hint of sadness and embarrassment. She looked around the room and sighed. At last she spoke, "I'm sorry. It's not mine anymore, and I seem to forget that from time to time. My husband and I did build it with a lot of love. We spent a few very happy years in this house, Mr. Ray. We used to live here, away from the madness of the city. We used to grow our own vegetables, run our own dairy, the local villagers respected us, our daughter was born in a room upstairs. We were very happy."

She paused, as if trying to remember some of her good times spent in this very room. "But then, I should have known. Good times never last long. My husband was diagnosed with cancer. I tried to save him. I did everything I could, but he was taken away from me."

"I'm sorry to hear that, Mrs. Chaudhuri," I said softly.

Nandita Chaudhuri looked dazed and lost in thought. She had grief written all over her face, as if the mask of serenity and composure that she otherwise wore, had suddenly dropped off. I could imagine why. It must be difficult for her to come back to the house which had her late husband's memories strewn all around. It must be more difficult to take care of that house, knowing it wasn't hers anymore.

Mrs. Chaudhuri finally shook herself out of her grief, and became as her calm and composed self again. She smiled apologetically. "Please pardon me, I didn't mean to ruin your evening."

"Not at all, Mrs. Chaudhuri. In fact, it's a pleasure knowing someone who's so brave." I meant that with all honesty.

Mrs. Chaudhuri held her head upright, and her jaws hardened. As I watched her expressions, I realized that somewhere, behind those calm, motherly features, there was a woman with a lot of angst. I didn't know what to do or say, and was quite relieved to see that Rajendra Mukherjee had walked up to us.

"Mrs. Chaudhuri, I see you have caught up with my dear nephew?" he asked with a smile on his face.

"I was telling Mrs. Chaudhuri what a beautiful house this is."

"Oh, Prakash, you should have seen it before I bought it. It was a beautiful nest, so to speak, complete in all aspects. And of course, as a star attraction, there used to be this lovely rose garden in the north-east corner of the compound, and Mrs. Chaudhuri used to take such good care of it. I had no idea that there could be so many varieties of roses and such different colours. She still takes such good care of this house. Without her, this would be merely an artist's den."

Nandita Chaudhuri didn't comment. She just smiled and changed the topic. The three of us spoke for some time, after which Mrs. Chaudhuri excused herself. Janardan Maity and Animesh Sen walked up to where Mr. Mukherjee and I were standing.

"Johnny, I kept thinking about that mate," said Mr. Mukherjee, "and I realized I could have avoided it."

"You can't retrace your path in chess and war, my friend. That's the name of the game. But yes, your knight took a few wrong turns that day," agreed his friend.

"My knight, ah yes, my knight . . ." Mr. Mukherjee said thoughtfully.

Janardan Maity turned to me. "Mr. Ray—"

"Please," I said. "Call me Prakash."

Janardan Maity smiled. "All right, Prakash. Do you play chess?"

"I used to, but I haven't played in some time."

"But you do enjoy it, don't you?"

"Oh yes, by all means, I enjoy it very much."

"Good. Your uncle and I are addicted to it. Animesh here, on the other hand, is more of a bridge person."

Animesh Sen nodded. "I can't go through a weekend without a game."

"We should play both games tomorrow," suggested Mr. Mukherjee, as he rubbed his hands enthusiastically. "Prakash, will you join us?"

"I'd love to."

"Good. Now, if you guys will please excuse Johnny and

me, we have a few things to discuss. Johnny, you want to come into the study?"

I looked around the room and noticed that Nandita Chaudhuri was now sitting on a sofa and having a conversation with Mrs. Mukherjee.

Just then I heard Animesh Sen ask, "I need a smoke, you mind stepping out into the veranda for a few minutes?"

"In this weather?" I asked.

"Come on, we'll be back in two minutes. I don't want to smoke inside the house."

The weather outside had shown no signs of improving. In fact, it had worsened. The rain was lashing its way halfway into the covered veranda, and it was biting cold, to boot. We pressed our backs to the wall and sheltered ourselves as much as possible. Animesh Sen offered me a cigarette. When I refused, he lit one himself, and after a couple of puffs, asked me over the howling wind, "So, you're a journalist?"

I said I was.

"Which paper?"

"I'm a freelancer."

"I see."

"How long have you known Mr. Mukherjee?" I asked him.

"Ever since he returned from Europe."

"And you manage his legal affairs?"

Animesh Sen nodded and puffed away at his cigarette. The rain lashed away at the width of the veranda and every now and then, there were flashes of lightning in the distant sky. For almost a minute or so, Animesh Sen didn't speak. Finally, almost in a bid to break the uncomfortable silence, I said,

"This is a lovely house and the location is very beautiful and refreshing."

"Too secluded for my taste. Too many problems, if you ask me. The nearest hospital is more than forty kilometres away. The roads aren't good either. And no restaurants. No cell phone reception."

I didn't respond. Clearly, here was a city man. There was nothing wrong with that though. His love for the urban way of life was as natural and as important as mine for the countryside. I waited for him to continue the conversation. But for several minutes, he kept puffing away. The wind was blowing hard and every now and then, it shook me to my bones. Finally, Animesh Sen spoke.

"Your uncle's got a bee in his bonnet."

The statement came so unexpectedly that I was taken aback. I said in an impulse, "Excuse me?"

"You heard it. The old man's going crazy."

"How do you mean?"

"Well, they say all artists are crazy. But this buff is beating his own kind by a fair margin."

"Why do you say so?"

"I have several reasons to say what I'm saying."

"Like what?" My voice was composed and the tone firm. Animesh Sen must have sensed that too.

He looked at me sternly for a few seconds and then said, "You see that pretty face flirting with him? She must be a third of his age."

"You mean Preeti? But he said she was like a . . ."

"Oh, come on!" Animesh Sen didn't make any effort to hide his irritation anymore. "Mr. Ray, one of the things I have learnt in my profession is that the eyes always take precedence over the ears. If you see something, forget about what you hear to the contrary. I'm not a child, you know," he said quite angrily, "nor am I blind."

I didn't know what to say.

"I don't like that secretary of his either," he went on.

"Who, Arun? But he seemed like a good man to me."

Animesh Sen turned towards me and asked, "Why?"

I was stumped. "I . . . why? What do you mean why?"

"Why did he seem like a good man to you, may I ask?"

"Well, he is quite intelligent, and is devoted to Mr. Mukherjee, and—"

"How did you arrive at that conclusion?"

"Mr. Mukherjee himself—"

"And you believed him?"

"I-I don't know . . . I didn't see any reason not to."

Animesh Sen threw the cigarette butt out into the rain in desperation. He didn't say anything for some time, and paced up and down the veranda, as if something was bothering him. Finally, he stopped in front of me, and said, "Look, Mr. Ray. You come across to me as a good man. Try and talk some sense into your uncle."

I listened silently, as he went on. "Tell him that he is not in Europe anymore. Tell him that at his age, he ought to be more careful, perhaps more religious. He has amassed a lot of wealth, you know? People will flock around him and be nice and sweet to him. But he must know his true friends from the opportunists. Because, when he is at his weakest, his so-called 'good friends' won't hesitate to—"

Animesh Sen stopped suddenly. I looked at him. His eyes had become narrow and he was looking at a distance, into the dark, rainy night. There was a strange expression of amazement on his face. Then he spoke, and three words escaped his lips, almost in a whisper, "What is that?"

As he uttered those words, I followed his gaze and looked out into the night, towards the gate of the perimeter fence. At first I could see nothing. It was like staring into the void. The gate itself was at least two hundred metres away, and thanks to the overcast sky and heavy rain, it was almost pitch dark. Then gradually, a dark shadowy form began to take shape.

I tried to take a step back, but I was already against the wall. The night was extremely cold now, and the chilly wind was almost unbearable. The shadowy form was getting bigger, and I soon realized that it was because it was moving towards us. I tried to look harder, and eventually I realized that the phantom-like shadow was actually the outline of a human being.

More specifically, it was a man.

"Who could it be, in this frightful weather?" I asked Animesh Sen.

"I have no idea," he replied.

The man was loitering down the pathway quite casually, as if not bothered by the weather at all. He was a tall man, probably middle-aged, and quite well built. He didn't seem to have an umbrella, and as he drew closer, I realized he was not wearing a raincoat either. Just a pair of jeans and a jacket. He was now fifteen feet from where we stood. Drenched from head to toe, his bloodshot eyes carried a calm yet lifeless expression.

The man walked up to where I was standing, and looked at me for a few seconds. His manner seemed extremely rough and uncivilized to me. He asked me in a gruff tone, "Who the hell are you?"

I was quite taken aback by his rude manner of speaking, and said, "I'm Prakash Ray, Mr. Mukherjee's nephew."

"Nephew?" the stranger said with a scoff. "I never knew my father had a nephew."

More Conversations

"Come inside, Narendra," said Animesh Sen. "Your father is waiting for you."

Narendra Mukherjee threw another despising look in my direction and walked past me to enter the house. Animesh Sen, silently gesturing for me to come in, followed him.

I stood in the veranda for some time, wondering what a strange man my cousin was. He didn't seem the least bit bothered by the weather and had literally strolled down from the main gate to the veranda. His manners were pretty ruffian too and in sharp contrast to those of his father's. To top it, he was drunk. I had smelled alcohol on him as he had walked past me.

The wind, which was pricking me like icicles now, stopped me from pondering further. I went inside and saw Mr. Mukherjee sitting on the couch with a frown on his grave face. He was obviously unhappy to see his son come to his party all drunk, soiled, and messed up.

Janardan Maity, who sat next to him, now walked up to me and said, "Prakash, perhaps you'll be kind enough to go in and bring your cousin back to the party after he's dried himself up?"

"Sure," I said. "Just tell me where to find him."

"His room's on this floor itself. Before you enter the dining room, take a right, and you'll see two rooms one after the other. The second room down the corridor is Narendra's. You'll find him there."

A minute or so later, I found myself knocking on the prescribed door.

"It's open," came the gruff voice from inside.

I entered the room and found Narendra Mukherjee drying himself with a towel. A small bottle of alcohol on the table caught my attention.

"What do you want?" came the angry question.

"They're waiting for you to come back to the party."

"Yeah, all right. But what do *you* want?"

"Me? I just came to fetch you . . ."

"That's not what I asked. Why are you *here*? In this blasted house?"

I hesitated for a moment, and then made up my mind. There was no reason I should have to tolerate such rude behaviour from this man. In a stern voice I said, "Please join the party when you are ready," and left the room.

As I exited, I met Preeti in the corridor. She peaked her eyebrows at me. "Did you just meet your cousin?"

I nodded.

"Jolly good weather for a couple of drinks, no? I can't say I blame him," she whispered, with a smile on her face.

I smiled politely to avoid a comment.

"You work for the papers, don't you? Do you write about any particular field?"

"Well, no. I generally cover book launches and press conferences, that sort of thing."

"You should do a story on your uncle. Don't you think it's sad that no one knows that such a famous man is living here in these woods?"

"I guess so," I said, "although I'll need to check with my editors first."

Preeti smiled. I couldn't help but notice that she was breathtakingly beautiful. She had large bright eyes and long flowing hair. Her lips were slender and her skin was absolutely flawless. She looked at me for some time and then said, "I don't know if I should be telling you this, but I don't like that cousin of yours very much. You would do well to steer clear of him."

For a few seconds I didn't know what to say. Finally I asked, "Why do you say so?"

She shrugged her shoulders in true French style. "Well, I know it's none of my business, but Mr. Mukherjee is quite upset with him. You see, during the course of my interviews, I sometimes ask him personal questions. I wouldn't be able to write a biography if I do not get to know the man behind the artist, right?"

"Yes, I see what you mean."

"Right, so whenever I ask him about his son, he seems to want to avoid such questions. He is quite bitter about him. And why wouldn't he be? I mean, look what he did today. Coming to his father's birthday party drunk to his gills! I feel sorry for Mr. Mukherjee."

Partly because I was curious, and partly because I wanted to avoid the uncomfortable discussion that was taking shape, I squeezed in a question: "Tell me something. Mr. Mitra told me that my uncle left the country in the early seventies, and that he returned only five years ago. So, how and where did he meet his first wife? I believe she was from Kolkata itself. Am I right?"

Preeti nodded. "Let me explain. Come, we'll sit here." We had walked back into the main hall by then, and as we took our seats, she began. "All right, since this is like a story, I'll tell it to you like one. You'll have to bear with me."

This brought a smile to my lips. "Go ahead."

Preeti passed her long and nimble fingers through a lock of hair that had fallen on her cheeks and pulled it behind her ears. Then she began her story. "In 1976, Barrister Nirmal Chakraborty of Bhowanipore sent his only child Aparna to study in Oxford. Aparna was a brilliant student and an excellent swimmer. One morning she was taking a stroll by the Thames, as was her daily habit, and your uncle walked up to her and introduced himself. He had already begun to taste some amount of success in the world of art by then. He requested Aparna to be his model for a portrait, but she respectfully declined. But artists are strange people, and your uncle surely is. For two months he pursued Aparna with steadfast devotion, explaining to her that if he would paint her portrait, it would be one of the best of his works. Finally, Aparna gave in and posed for him. She was later mesmerized by her own portrait. By this time, they had fallen in love with each other and roughly a year later they got married in London itself. Needless to say, Barrister Chakraborty was not one bit happy about this, and vowed not to see his daughter's face ever again. But when three years later, Aparna sent a photo of little Narendra playing in Hampstead Heath to her father, he wrote back saying that he longed to see his little grandson, and that she and her husband had all his blessings."

"Wow," I said as Preeti paused. "What a fascinating story!"

"Oh yes," she agreed. "Just wait till the book comes out. Your uncle's life is *very* interesting."

"It's really wonderful that you're writing about him."

Preeti smiled. "You should too."

I smiled back, and looked at her eyes. They were beautiful. I scavenged for words. I needed to say something.

"Do you know where Arun is? I need to speak to him," I somehow said.

"Why yes, I had seen him here some time back. Let me think. Hmmm . . . aah yes, I think he went to your uncle's study to make a call. Oh no no, I then saw him going into his own room."

"Okay, I think I should go speak to him, if you'll excuse me."

"Sure, let's catch up again soon, though. Oh, by the way, do you know your way around the house?"

"No, can't say I do. I just got here like an hour ago."

"No worries, I'll guide you. Go straight from here, and turn left. Take the corridor on the other side of the dining room. Arun's room is the third door on the left."

"Thanks, Preeti." I somehow managed to say and then went and knocked on the door of Arun Mitra's room.

Arun Mitra was at his desk, writing something in his diary. He said, "Oh there you are! I was looking for you. Is everything all right?"

"Umm . . . yes. I was just having a conversation with Preeti and she told me an interesting story about Mr. Mukherjee," I remarked.

"Yeah, she knows a lot about him now."

"Is that so . . .?" I hesitated.

"She has to, it's her job," Arun said nonchalantly.

I wanted to confirm what Animesh Sen had told me but I figured Arun Mitra, the devoted secretary, was the last person I should put such a question to. Moreover, I had been in the house only for a few hours. I figured it wouldn't be wise to meddle in such matters. Instead, I asked, "Did you know that Narendra has come in?"

"Yes, Mrs. Mukherjee told me."

"He seemed . . ."

"Yes, we were expecting it," he said, ever so calmly.

The house seemed full of strange characters. My head was all jumbled up, thinking of all the people I had met throughout the evening. But, somehow, I liked the efficient and devoted Arun Mitra the most, perhaps because of his affable nature.

I chatted with him for some more time. We spoke about my job and his poetry and the weather and such other things. Then he showed me to my room upstairs. Like the rest of the house, it was a neatly maintained room. The bed was comfortable and there was an attached bathroom. Arun Mitra left me in my room, saying, "I'm sure you'll want to take a wash and rest for some time. Dinner will be served at nine o'clock sharp."

After he left, I peeped into the bathroom and was relieved to see that it had a geyser. I took a nice warm wash, changed into a clean pair of clothes, and lay down on the bed for some time. My mind was trying to sort through all the information it had received in such a short span of time. I wondered what Animesh Sen was talking about. Clearly, he was worried about something. Did he have any reason to suspect that Mr. Mukherjee was in danger? I remembered he was my uncle's legal advisor. In that capacity, he may have a lot of information to my uncle's financial affairs. But why was he referring to Preeti and saying such things about her? And Arun Mitra seemed such a nice person to me—why did Animesh Sen say he didn't like him?

***

Dinner was an elaborate affair. Mrs. Mukherjee once again proved to be the perfect hostess. She kept an eye out for everyone's needs and passed on second helpings herself. My uncle seemed to be in a good mood. Janardan Maity sat on his left and Preeti on his right. He conversed with them in turns and seemed to be happy that everyone was together. The fact that his son had been missing at the table didn't seem to bother him, at least momentarily. I figured he realized that he was better off in his room in his inebriated condition, than at the table. There were remarks about the weather—the storm howled on—and plans for the next day were discussed. I was seated next to Devendra Mukherjee and we spoke briefly.

"Raja tells me about your mother. Sadly, I don't seem to remember her at all," Devendra Mukherjee remarked in a conversational manner.

"You must be quite a few years younger than your brother?" I asked.

"Yes, almost fourteen years. And you're right, that could explain why I don't remember her."

"Where do you live in Kolkata?"

"Salt Lake. And you?"

"Ballygunge."

"That's a nice locality."

"Arun was telling me that Mr. & Mrs. Mukherjee sometimes live in the city."

"Yes, Raja visits the National Library twice every month. He has a flat somewhere near Minto Park, although I don't know where exactly. When he comes to the city, he stays there."

"You don't get to meet him often, it seems?"

"I leave home for the hospital early in the morning. I also run a clinic in the evening. I hardly get any time."

"I see . . ."

"You're a journalist?"

"Umm . . . yes. I'm more of a freelancer, really."

The small talk didn't proceed further. I was never good at conversations, and Devendra Mukherjee seemed like a reticent man too.

After dinner, everyone except Nandita Chaudhuri gathered in the main hall. She said she had to make a phone call and went into Mr. Mukherjee's study.

Mrs. Mukherjee walked up to me and held my hand. "I can't tell you how sorry I am. I haven't had an opportunity to have a chat with you. Won't you sit down with me here? Raja speaks very fondly of your mother. Her name was Suhasini, right?"

"Yes," I replied, "I believe they were pretty close as cousins."

"Oh yes. Raja doesn't make friends very easily. But once he does, he really commits himself to the friendship. He told me some of the most wonderful things about your mother."

I smiled proudly. I had never seen my mother but was quite used to hearing wonderful things being said about her. I had a sudden urge to ask Mrs. Mukherjee about the letter—the one that Mr. Mukherjee had spoken about earlier—but I restrained myself and decided to wait. After all, Mr. Mukherjee had promised to show the letter to me.

"Have you met any of the guests earlier, before tonight, I mean?" she asked, as she indicated towards the people in the hall.

"No, I haven't."

"All very lovely people, really, aren't they?"

I looked at her. She was still smiling, but had cast a loaded glance towards the far end of the room. I realized she was referring to Preeti, who was seated on the sofa along with Mr. Mukherjee. They seemed to be enjoying a hearty laughter. I also noticed that Animesh Sen stood alone at a distance, and was stealing furtive glances at them.

I felt quite embarrassed and uncomfortable. I tried to look for a change of topic for our conversation, but was at a loss of words. Mrs. Mukherjee sighed and finally turned to me.

"So, Prakash, how do you like the countryside?" she asked.

I was much relieved and replied quickly. "Well, I grew up in a small town. So, I don't feel like a fish out of water, for sure."

"I see what you mean. For some people, though, this may seem like living in the wilderness. Animesh, for instance. He keeps telling me that I am better off in the city. I was born and brought up in the heart of London city, you see? But I quite like it here; at least it breaks the monotony of a one-track existence. Even when we were growing up in London, my parents used to take all the children to my aunt's farmhouse in the country. We have spent a lot of time there."

"The house is beautiful," I said.

"Oh yes, Nandita takes good care of the house. It's a pity she had to sell it after the accident, but we're so glad that she comes by often. Because whenever she does, the house almost gets a makeover of sorts."

"You have a flat in the city, don't you?"

"Yes. I live there most of the time. I usually come here over the weekends. But of late, I have found myself spending more time here. Raja hasn't been keeping very well."

A strong bolt of lightning struck somewhere close by with an ominous crackling sound, generating gasps of various sizes and tones from everyone in the hall. The glass panes rattled vigorously and the chandelier started swinging just a wee bit, making our shadows oscillate around the hall.

"Pretty ghastly weather!" I remarked.

"Yes. I hope poor Mahadev is all right in his cottage," she said with concern.

Just then Nandita Chaudhuri walked into the room and on seeing Mrs. Mukherjee sitting with me, she walked up to us.

"Made your call?" Mrs. Mukherjee asked and held out a hand to her.

"Yes," Nandita Chaudhuri said. "I was actually supposed to be back in the city tonight. But this storm . . ."

"Rubbish!" said Mrs. Mukherjee, as she tugged at her hand and made Mrs. Chaudhuri sit next to her. "Storm or no storm, I wouldn't have let you go tonight. Raja and I have planned a nice party for tomorrow."

Nandita Chaudhuri smiled in response, then asked, "Where's Narendra?"

"He must be in his room. I'll go see him after some time. He hasn't had his dinner yet."

Scattered conversations took place for some more time. Various people came up to me and chatted. Throughout these conversations, nature continued to wreak havoc outside the bungalow, but other than making one or two conversational remarks about the weather, no one paid any attention to the repeated premonitions of the calamity that was to strike the Mukherjee bungalow later that night.

Murder

At around half past ten, as I was speaking to Animesh Sen, I noticed Mrs. Mukherjee come out of the dining room with a covered tray in her hands and walk towards the corridor. Dinner for the drunk, I figured. It was nice to see that although her stepson didn't think much of her, Mrs. Mukherjee had not forgotten her duties.

Animesh Sen still seemed upset about how freely Preeti and my uncle were talking to each other, throwing stern glances at them every now and then. Almost in a bid to put his mind at ease, I asked him about his father. The trick seemed to work, because he spoke at length about his father and his friendship with Mr. Mukherjee. "I was very close to my father, Mr. Ray," he eventually said, "and he was very fond of your uncle. It's not without reason that I'm worried about him."

"What exactly are you worried about?" I finally asked.

Mr. Sen hesitated. He obviously had something in his mind, but he was not letting it show, or talking about it. What was most surprising to me was the fact that he was confiding in me in such a matter. He obviously knew other people in the room much better and for a longer period of time. Why was he telling me?

The conversation could not continue because my uncle and Janardan Maity joined us.

"I'm so happy you came, Prakash. Are you enjoying yourself?" my uncle asked.

I told him how lonely my usual weekends were and what a great party this was. Janardan Maity had just made a comment on how a reader is never alone and begun to elucidate his point, when suddenly, he seemed to have seen something and his face turned grave. I turned around to see what the matter was and saw Arun Mitra staggering into the hall from around the corner. His face had become almost white—as if he had seen a ghost. His hands and legs were trembling and if Devendra Mukherjee had not rushed to his side and grabbed him, he would have surely collapsed on the floor. We rushed to the spot on the floor where Devendra Mukherjee had made him sit.

Mr. Rajendra Mukherjee anxiously brushed past everyone and knelt beside Arun, who was still in a state of shock.

"What happened to you, Arun? Are you okay? What happened?" he asked.

Arun looked up at his master's face in a trance, and stared into it for several seconds. Slowly, an expression of horror descended upon his face and with great effort, in an almost unrecognizable voice, he somehow managed to speak a few words: "Mrs. . . . . . Mukherjee . . . . . corridor . . ."

Devendra Mukherjee immediately ran towards the corridor that led to the interior of the house. An expression of horror and a fear for the obvious crept into the already anxious face of Rajendra Mukherjee. He struggled to get up on his feet, and once he managed to stand up, he tried to run towards the corridor. Janardan Maity screamed at him, "No, Mukherjee!" Then he tugged at my arm and whispered into my ear, "Stay with your uncle. Don't leave his side, no matter what," and made a dash towards the corridor.

I held my uncle's hand as he staggered, his legs clearly failing him. I put his arm around my shoulder to support him. We turned around the corner and stepped into the corridor.

I will try to describe the sight that met my eyes when I entered the corridor.

The corridor was quite wide, almost seven-eight feet wide. There was only one door to the left, which led to the kitchen. This door was now shut. On the right, there were two doors, one after the other. I knew about the last door, the one farthest from the spot where I was standing—that door opened into Narendra Mukherjee's room. After crossing that room, the corridor continued for another six feet or so, before it took a sharp turn to the left and disappeared into the interior of the bungalow. It was at this turn, that I saw a pair of legs on the floor, peeping out of the corner. The colour of the churidaar was unmistakable. I had heard Nandita Chaudhuri admire Mrs. Mukherjee's dress less than an hour ago. One of the sandals had come off her feet, the other still managed to cling on to her big toe. She seemed to be lying on her back. Janardan Maity was standing next to the body with a grimace on his face and I heard Devendra Mukherjee's voice say, "No, she's dead."

As soon as I heard those words, the weight on my shoulder

suddenly felt very heavy. I realized that my uncle was about to collapse. He was at least a good one foot taller than me. I struggled to hold him upright and shouted out for Janardan Maity, who rushed to my aid. Together, we carried my uncle to the nearest room on the right and lay him down on a couch. In the meantime Animesh Sen rushed to the spot and let out a sharp gasp of shock and horror. He guided the two ladies into the room. Janardan Maity entrusted Nandita Chaudhuri and Preeti with the task of taking care of my uncle, and rushed back to the main hall to check on Arun. Animesh Sen stayed back in the room with the ladies. I, on the other hand, nervously stepped out to the corridor and walked up to the body.

It was a nasty sight. She had been stabbed on her chest with a sharp instrument, although the weapon itself was nowhere to be seen. Her yellow dress was soaked in blood. Her face had contorted in the shock and horror that must have befallen her in her last moments, and turned towards the right, facing one of the walls of the passage. Her eyes were lifeless, and her entire body was twisted beyond decorum. Devendra Mukherjee had given up and was sitting next to the body on the floor with his head hanging in frustration. My legs were trembling. Devendra Mukherjee was a doctor and he may have seen a sight like this several times, but I had never seen anything like this before.

Devendra Mukherjee looked at me and said, "Strange! She's been dead about half an hour or so! When did you last see her?"

"I . . . I saw her taking Narendra's dinner to his room."

Devendra Mukherjee stared at me for some time, as his jaws tightened. He pulled himself up from the floor and took a few seconds to steady himself. Then he looked around and pulled out the curtain from one of the windows with a sharp jerk and covered the corpse with it. He took a deep breath and said to me, "Come with me, and be careful."

As I heard those two words—*"be careful"*—a very terrifying realization gradually began to dawn on me, although the very idea seemed shocking to me. Narendra Mukherjee!? Did he . . .? But surely, that was impossible!

Devendra Mukherjee walked up to Narendra's room, and I followed him. Very cautiously, he turned the knob of Narendra's door clockwise and pushed the door inside. It opened with a slow creak. He waited, with his back to the wall next to the door. My heart seemed to beat so fast that I was afraid that it would burst. The room was dark, and Devendra Mukherjee and I hesitated to enter. We exchanged meaningful glances, made up our minds, nodded at each other and were just about to enter, when we were startled by Janardan Maity who had dashed around the corner and almost collided with us.

"The phone is out!" he panted for breath, and Devendra Mukherjee and I immediately shushed him to keep his voice down. I gestured towards the dark room, but Janardan Maity seemed confused.

In a sudden move, Devendra Mukherjee hurled himself through the door and turned on the lights. I entered the room with Janardan Maity peeping over my shoulders. My heart pounding inside my chest, I saw a strange sight inside the room. Right next to the table lamp, which now filled the room with light, was the covered tray which the poor woman had brought in for her stepson. It was obvious that the tray had not been touched after it had been set down on the table. On the bedside table, the bottle of alcohol I had seen earlier now stood empty, along with a wristwatch and a wallet. But most important of all, right ahead of us, on the bed, sat Narendra Mukherjee, in an obviously inebriated condition. His eyes were red, he seemed out of breath, and his mouth was almost frothing.

"Get out of my room! All of you. Get out!" he snarled, like a cornered animal which bares its teeth when threatened.

Janardan Maity tugged at my shirt and pointed at the floor. I looked down and saw that a thin trail of drops of blood had started from the doorway, moving towards the bed, and finally disappearing below it. Devendra Mukherjee had seen it too. In a swift move, Janardan Maity picked up the table lamp and put it on the floor, near the bed. We went down on the floor and looked under the bed. Although an obviously hurried attempt had been made to conceal it by throwing it under the bed, a blood-stained dagger was now revealed by the bright light.

We had found the murder weapon.

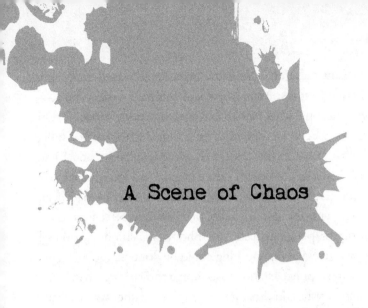

A Scene of Chaos

Over the next one hour, several things happened, and the house was a scene of utter chaos, to say the least. But several people pitched in to bring back whatever little order was possible, given the circumstances.

Nandita Chaudhuri had seemed to me as a strong-willed woman; it was nice to see that I was not mistaken. She did not let Mr. Mukherjee anywhere near his wife's corpse. Although the latter pleaded with Mrs. Chaudhuri, and then Devendra Mukherjee, to be allowed to catch one last glimpse of his wife, his brother was stern. "You don't want to remember her like that for the rest of your life, do you? Your heart is weak. You'll go upstairs and lie down on your bed, right now."

Animesh Sen and Devendra Mukherjee took him upstairs. Then Animesh Sen ran out in the rain and called Mahadev into the bungalow from

73

the servant quarters. Nandita Chaudhuri stayed with Mr. Mukherjee upstairs. Arun Mitra had received a rude shock— he was the one who had discovered the body after all. On Preeti's instructions, Mahadev gave him a glass of hot milk, and he sat down in the main hall, accompanied by her. I had not seen Janardan Maity for a considerable period of time, and on asking Devendra Mukherjee, found out that he had been entrusted with the responsibility of confining Narendra to his room till the police arrived. The phone was still not working, and it was decided that nothing could be done till the morning. The nearest police station was apparently more than sixty kilometres away, and driving there in this weather was virtually impossible. I went up to my uncle's room with Devendra Mukherjee, and found him in a pretty bad shape. Even in this chilly weather, he was perspiring heavily. Devendra Mukherjee checked his pulse and his face turned grave. He gave his brother an injection and said, "This will help you sleep, and that is what you need the most right now. Mrs. Chaudhuri, will you please switch off the light?"

We came downstairs and found everyone assembled in the main hall. Arun Mitra, Preeti, Animesh Sen, Devendra Mukherjee, Nandita Chaudhuri, and myself—all were present. Mahadev stood in one corner with his hands folded and with tears in his eyes. Narendra, who had been escorted by Janardan Maity to the hall, was now sitting on a single chair. I remembered I had sat in that chair earlier today, when I had entered the bungalow for the first time. As soon as Mrs. Chaudhuri saw Narendra, she asked him in a cold voice, "What had she done to you? Why did you kill her?"

"Be careful, Mrs. Chaudhuri, we don't know that for sure," said Devendra Mukherjee in a calm yet steely voice that was heard by all. There was a stunned silence in the room, and everyone's eyes were fixed on him.

The storm was still raging on outside and flashes of lightning came in through the glass windowpanes, making the room look scary. Everyone realized that a terrible and nasty crime had just been committed, and everyone seemed to have a pretty good idea as to who could have done it. But for some strange reason, Devendra Mukherjee seemed to be opposing the idea.

"What are you talking about? You said you found the bloody knife under his bed, didn't you?" asked Mrs. Chaudhuri. She was obviously not happy with what Devendra Mukherjee was saying.

"Yes, we did find the knife. But that doesn't mean he killed Anita," he said equanamiously.

Animesh Sen said, "Then who killed her?"

"I don't know," said Devendra Mukherjee as he poured himself a glass of water.

"What do you mean you don't know?" asked Animesh Sen, in an angry tone.

"I mean I don't know, Animesh. I'm not saying Narendra didn't kill Anita. Perhaps he did. But we can't say for sure, can we?"

"Of course we can!"

Devendra Mukherjee looked at him with a grave face and said, "You are a lawyer, aren't you? I don't know how you can say something like that. In fact, I have a few questions in my mind which keep bothering me."

"Questions? What questions?"

Devendra Mukherjee took his time to drink the water. Everyone in the room looked at him. It was quite obvious that no one had liked what he had said. Finally, he said, "Several questions come to my mind. For instance, *why* would Narendra murder his stepmother? What was the motive?"

Nandita Chaudhuri said, "Well, we all know he couldn't tolerate her. She had taken his mother's place after all."

Devendra Mukherjee paced up and down the room. "Yes, I am aware of that. But is that strong enough reason for him to kill her? Moreover, if he did kill her, would he make the mistake of killing her right outside his room? And then carry the dagger all the way and hide it under his bed?"

"He was drunk, for god's sake!" retorted Animesh Sen, in an agitated voice.

Devendra Mukherjee didn't respond immediately. He frowned deeply, and seemed to be lost in some faraway thought. For quite some time, no one spoke. I was noticing Narendra. He sat in his chair and stared at the floor, still in his drunken stupor, still fuming.

After almost two minutes, Devendra Mukherjee said, "May I ask you a question?"

I looked at him and realized that his question was directed at Animesh Sen. Everyone's eyes turned towards Animesh, who hesitated for some time. He licked his lips, straightened his jacket, and finally said, "Wh . . . what question?"

"When you went out to call Mahadev through the back door, was it locked?"

Animesh Sen stared back at Devendra Mukherjee with a fixed gaze for some time before saying, "Yes, bolted from the inside."

Devendra Mukherjee nodded. "There are only two exits from this bungalow. We were all present in this hall when the murder happened. And we didn't see anyone come in or go out through the main door. That leaves the rear exit, which according to Animesh, was bolted from inside too."

"What is your point?" asked Nandita Chaudhuri.

Devendra Mukherjee did not answer at once, but when he did answer, his voice was steely cold. "My point, Mrs. Chaudhuri, is that the murderer is still in this room."

Alibis

For a few seconds, no one spoke. We looked at each other's faces in turns, almost as if we were trying to look for signs that would expose the murderer. Finally, Preeti said, "Isn't that obvious? Of course the murderer is in this room. He is sitting in that chair over there" and pointed towards Narendra.

Devendra Mukherjee raised his hands. "Come now, I am saying this again, let's not jump to conclusions so quickly and start accusing people. I don't think we have enough reason to believe that Narendra committed the murd—"

Before Devendra Mukherjee could complete his sentence, Animesh Sen jumped in. "You are saying that because he is your nephew," he said. Then he turned towards the rest of us and said, "Don't you see? Isn't it natural for him to try and protect his nephew?"

Although no one spoke, all eyes turned towards Devendra Mukherjee, who shrugged his shoulders. "Why? Why would I try to protect him?"

Animesh Sen continued to argue. "There could be several reasons. You have known Narendra for a long time now. It's been several years that he has been in the city. For all we know, you and he go to the same club. Perhaps . . . perhaps he looked up to you. Perhaps you were more of a father to him than your brother ever was."

Devendra Mukherjee grimaced. "What nonsense are you talking about?"

"Well then," Preeti interrupted, "who do *you* think is the murderer?"

"Look, I don't claim to know who the murderer is. I simply—"

Animesh Sen interjected again, this time in a sarcastic voice. "Oh yeah? I thought you were the big detective here. Asking questions and making inferences and conclusions and all that. Why don't you tell us something . . . where were *you* when the murder took place, eh?"

Devendra Mukherjee looked at Animesh Sen in a composed manner and said, "I was having a conversation with Mrs. Chaudhuri."

All eyes turned towards Nandita Chaudhuri, who confirmed it. "Yes, what he is saying is true. We were having a conversation about tomorrow's party."

I hadn't said anything so far, but now I felt I should chip in too. I did not like the way Devendra Mukherjee was being harassed. Had it not been for him, things would have been much worse in this house tonight. "I can vouch for that too," I said.

Everyone looked at me.

I continued. "At around 10:30 p.m., I saw Mrs. Mukherjee take Narendra's dinner to his room. From that time onwards till the body was discovered, Dr. Mukherjee was in this room, having a conversation with Mrs. Chaudhuri."

"All right, all right," Animesh Sen raised both his hands in the air and said impatiently. "So the two of them were here. And I was talking to Prakash and Mr. Mukherjee and Mr. Maity. Where were you, Preeti?"

Preeti was startled and visibly at a loss for words. It was then that Arun Mitra spoke. "She was with me."

"Yes," said Preeti quickly. "I was with Arun."

"So, it seems we are all accounted for," Animesh concluded. "The only person in this room whose whereabouts were unknown when the murder happened was Narendra."

Everyone was silent once again.

Animesh Sen yelled out in exasperation. "Oh come on, do you still need more proof? This man murdered his stepmother."

All of a sudden, before we could understand what happened, Narendra Mukherjee shot out from his chair like a dart and pounced upon Animesh Sen. The thing happened so quickly that we couldn't prevent Narendra from landing a nasty uppercut on Animesh Sen's left cheek. As Animesh Sen collapsed on the floor like a felled tree, both the ladies shrieked out. The first to dash in to control Narendra was Janardan Maity. Devendra Mukherjee and Arun Mitra also rushed to the spot and grabbed him, but it was proving difficult to contain him. He was of a large build and seemed to have the strength of an ox in him. He was trying to go for Animesh Sen's throat, although it was quite clear to us that he had been knocked out.

After a lot of struggle, Narendra seemed to back off, and was shoved into a chair. I was kneeling beside Animesh Sen and trying to shake him back to his senses. Devendra Mukherjee came to my aid. He sprinkled some water on his face and nursed him back to his senses. Observing the face, he said, "Thank goodness the punch hasn't cut him, but he will probably have a black eye in the morning." We helped Animesh Sen back on his feet. He covered his eye with his hand and sat down quietly between Arun Mitra and Preeti.

Devendra Mukherjee turned towards Narendra and said in a stern voice, "Narendra, I'm sure by now you have realized that everyone in this room is baying for your blood right now. And the only thing that is preventing them from going for your throat is me. But if you continue to act in such a foolish manner, you'll lose my sympathy too. So, you'll listen to me and stay calm till the police arrive. Can you do that for me?"

His words were spoken clearly and authoritatively. Narendra was still looking at Animesh Sen with bloodshot eyes and panting heavily. It seemed he would tear him apart with his teeth at the first opportunity.

"Can you do that for me?" Dr. Mukherjee's voice rose one scale above normal and rung through the hall.

Narendra broke eye contact with Animesh, nodded his head and slouched back in his chair.

"Good, now we are going to do things in an orderly fashion here tonight," demanded Devendra Mukherjee as he glanced at his watch. "Mrs. Chaudhuri, would you be so kind as to check on my brother upstairs? Mr. Maity, I'm leaving Narendra in your custody. Please see that he doesn't try his boxing tricks again. I'll check if the phone is working now. The rest of you please remain in this room."

Janardan Maity went and stood beside Narendra's chair. Nandita Chaudhuri was about to rise from her seat wearily when I walked up to her and said, "Mrs. Chaudhuri, why don't you sit? I'll go and check on him instead."

She gave a faint smile and plonked back down, and I proceeded to take the stairs to the first floor. What a nightmarish turn of events! The weather outside seemed like a menace, but it was nothing compared to what was happening inside the house. The murder seemed to have jolted each and every one out of their wits and brought out the ugly side in some. And here I was stuck in this mess. The vision of Mrs. Mukherjee's contorted face and the horrible sight of her eyeballs almost popping out of their sockets flashed in my mind and I shut my eyes tight. I had never seen a nastier sight. It seemed to me that more than the pain, the identity of the killer must have come as a violent shock to her. It was written all over her face.

I was exhausted, and my body was shivering. I realized that keeping with the need of the hour, I had done a lot of running around, but the shock of everything that was going on was finally catching up with me. My calf muscles were tired and aching and my throat was parched. I badly needed a glass of water. I remembered there was a jug of water placed in my room. I went up to my room first and poured myself a glass of water. Having quenched my thirst, I steadied myself for a few moments, and then emerged back into the passage and walked up to my uncle's room. I knew he would be asleep, so, I turned the doorknob softly and entered. It was quite dark inside. I remembered Mrs. Chaudhuri switching off the light before we left, so I decided not to switch it on, lest it wake the poor old man up. What he needed right now was the rest. What a nasty shock he had received, that too on such a special day!

I walked up by his bedside and strained my eyes to see if he was asleep. In the near-dark, I noticed that my uncle's eyes were shut. He seemed to be sleeping peacefully. I was relieved and tried to look for the edge of the blanket so that I could draw it over his chest. Right then, as I was hunched over him, there was a lightning outside, and in the flash of light that came in through the window and illuminated the bed momentarily, I saw a blood-stained dagger rising from his chest!

Accusations

I wouldn't be able to tell you much about what went on in my head in the few moments after I discovered that Rajendra Mukherjee had been murdered too. Honestly, I simply don't remember. I must have stayed in the room for a long time, because my legs had turned completely numb and I had barely any strength to move at all. After what seemed like an eternity to me, I managed to walk backwards and leave the room, without taking my eyes off the bed, for the fear of some unknown assailant driving a dagger through my chest too. I am ashamed to say that I was so afraid that I broke into a sweat in the middle of that cold January night.

Preeti was the first to see me as I walked back into the hall. She let out a short scream, and I realized my own face must have lost all colour, thanks to the horror I had experienced. Devendra Mukherjee and Janardan Maity ran up to me and asked me what had happened. I was in no position to respond, and I heard their footsteps dash up the staircase behind me. Arun Mitra and Animesh Sen ran up to me. I somehow managed to relate to them what I had seen upstairs. A chaotic scene of grief and tears ensued, the nature of which can be assessed when I say that I was left alone in the hall and everyone, including Narendra and Mahadev, dashed upstairs and for the next few minutes, blood curdling howls of sobbing were heard from my uncle's bedroom. My head was reeling and I collapsed on a couch.

Gradually, and I am not really sure after exactly how much time, everyone came downstairs one by one. All eyes were moist, and everyone, without exception, had been shocked and baffled beyond their wits to have witnessed two tragedies back to back on the same night. As for myself, I tried to muster all the courage I could, but as soon as I remembered that I was now stuck with a bunch of strangers inside a secluded bungalow hundred kilometres from home in the middle of a stormy night with two corpses and a murderer amongst us, I felt the pounding of my heart once again.

Someone among us had murdered Mr. Mukherjee and his wife. Who could have committed such a horrible and unthinkable crime? I looked around the room.

Preeti was weeping and Nandita Chaudhuri was patting her on her back in a bid to console her, although she herself seemed quite shocked. Devendra Mukherjee had sat down on a nearby chair and buried his face in his palms. Arun Mitra had almost collapsed on the sofa and Janardan Maity had poured a glass of water and was trying to make him drink it. Animesh Sen was standing near the window, with an expression of horror on his face. He tried to light a cigarette but his hands were trembling so much that he put it back in his pocket. Narendra sat on a chair, and stared at the floor in a daze.

I was just beginning to think that I had never in my life been in a situation like this before, and that things couldn't become any worse, when a question from Animesh Sen sent a cold shiver down my spine.

"When you found him, was he already dead?" I heard him ask me.

I could feel all the eyes in the room turn towards me. I stuttered, "Wh-what do you mean?"

"I'm not saying anything . . . I'm just—" began Animesh Sen.

Janardan Maity turned towards Animesh Sen and said calmly, "If you don't shut up, the next punch to land on your jaw will be mine."

"No, but he has a point," said Nandita Chaudhuri. "Am I the only one here who thinks he took a long time to check on Mr. Mukherjee and come back?"

I was trembling at the possibility these strange people were suggesting. Did they think I murdered Rajendra Mukherjee? Surely, they couldn't possibly be thinking on those lines. Could they? I . . . I had just met Rajendra Mukherjee for the first time in my life a few hours ago! I suddenly felt very sick. A lump seemed to churn within my stomach and struggle to find its way up my throat. My hands and feet began to tremble. I looked from one face to another, searching for some compassion, but I couldn't find any. Even Mahadev had stopped sobbing and was looking at me suspiciously.

Devendra Mukherjee lost his calm and said in an irritated voice, "For heaven's sake, what's wrong with you people? Let us all keep calm and stop making baseless allegations, please."

Animesh Sen, not one to back down easily, asserted, "No,

we ought to discuss this. I refuse to spend the night in the same room with two murderers."

Devendra Mukherjee protested again, and an argument ensued, much of which I did not even hear. My head was spinning. I had to do something . . . something . . . anything. Gathering all the strength I could, I picked myself up on my feet. Rain and storm be damned, I had to get out of this place. I staggered towards the door, overturning a bronze statue on a mantelpiece on my way, and just as I was about to reach the door, I was stopped by Janardan Maity.

He put a soft hand on my shoulder, looked straight into my eyes, and whispered under his breath, "My dear friend, sit down. What you are about to do is going to lead you into more trouble than you are in right now."

There was something in his voice—I can't explain it, really—which made me think I should listen to him. My uncle had said that he had a heart of gold. In a desperate effort to clutch at the only support in the room, I told Janardan Maity in a trembling voice, "I didn't kill him."

"All the more reason for you to sit down," Janardan Maity whispered in an assuring tone. "Please, sit down."

After he had made me sit down in a sofa, he turned around to the others and said, "I know we have all had an exceedingly tragic experience tonight. But I completely agree with Dr. Mukherjee. Please, let us not accuse each other. We have to wait for the police to arrive. Please sit down, all of you. I request you all to sit down."

Slowly, everyone took their seats around the hall. Janardan Maity poured me a glass of water. And as I drank it, I felt very uncomfortable, for I could feel all the prying eyes looking at me with nothing but suspicion.

"Did you try the phone, Dr. Mukherjee?" asked Janardan Maity.

"Yes . . . it's working now," said Devendra Mukherjee.

"And?"

"I called the police. They are on their way. I think we should stop quarrelling among ourselves and just wait for them to arrive."

"I agree," said Janardan Maity evenly. "We will now wait."

Nandita Chaudhuri suddenly lost her temper and shouted at the top of her voice, "What do you mean we will wait? What if the murderer is still in the house?"

"I assure you, Mrs. Chaudhuri," said Janardan Maity, as he sat down on the sofa next to me, "that the murderer is still in the house."

"How can you say that so calmly?" asked Preeti, "What if there's another murder?"

"Ms. Preeti, trust me when I tell you, that if everyone stays in this room till the police arrive, we shall all be safe."

Strange Questions

After almost three hours or so, the police arrived. In the course of these three hours, which seemed like the longest three hours of my life, none of us spoke. Furtive and suspicious glances were thrown at each other, and I myself did the same. I couldn't think straight and everyone seemed like a suspect. Several questions crowded around in my head, poking me from various directions. Did Narendra really kill Anita Mukherjee? If yes, why did he throw the blood-stained dagger under his bed? And if he killed his stepmother, then who killed his father? He was in this room all throughout. In fact, no one (other than me) had been upstairs after we had put my uncle to sleep and come downstairs. Who, then, stabbed Rajendra Mukherjee? And why?

The police examined the two bodies and carried out their procedures. The bodies were photographed and carried away. One by one we were asked to come into the dining room, where we were questioned separately. I was interrogated too, and I answered all the questions put to me to the best of my knowledge. The police also seemed to suspect me—two officers whispered to each other and kept staring at me for a long time, before finally letting me go, with the warning that I was not to leave the house till further instructions.

The morning came, and we were all allowed to go to our respective rooms. There was no question of sleeping, but I did lie down for some time. My life seemed to have turned upside down. To be honest, I was quite afraid. I didn't have much faith in the police and I was quite certain that they would do a half-baked job and arrest the most likely suspect in the matter. And I knew, without a grain of doubt in my mind, that the most likely suspect would be me. Because, none of the other people in the house had left the hall and been anywhere near my uncle as he slept upstairs. The only person who had been near him was I. And no matter how solemnly I was willing to swear that I did not kill him and that he was already dead when I found him, the police had nothing to go by but my own word for it. My head hurt at thinking of all the ominous possibilities that could follow in the next few hours. I began to realize that my life would never be the same again.

At around 8 o'clock in the morning, Janardan Maity came to my room with a few cookies on a plate.

"You will need all your strength this morning, Prakash. Do eat," he said.

I refused, saying I wasn't hungry, but he insisted. After I had eaten a couple of cookies, he gave me a glass of water and then said in a soft voice, "Now, Prakash. I know you are not in the right frame of mind. But we are running against time, you see? Would you mind if I ask you a few questions? Trust me, you have nothing to worry."

I had regained some of my strength in the morning light, and was able to gather my thoughts together. When I looked at his face, I realized that he was trying to help me, and I decided to answer his questions.

Janardan Maity said, "When I went up to your uncle's room after you had found out that he was murdered, I noticed that the light had been switched off and the room was dark. When you entered the room, was the light switched off or did you switch it off?"

"It was already switched off when I entered," I said.

"You mean to say that someone had switched it off before you entered the room?"

"Yes, it was switched off when we had put my uncle in bed."

"Do you know who switched it off?"

I thought for a moment and replied, "Mrs. Chaudhuri."

"When did she switch it off?"

"Before she left the room earlier last night. I was with her."

"I see. So, she was the last to leave the room?"

"Yes . . . no, we both left the room together."

"And why didn't you switch the light on when you entered the room later to check on your uncle?"

"I was afraid I might wake him up."

Janardan Maity frowned and seemed to be lost in some deep thought for a few seconds. Then, he pulled a chair close to the bed and sat down on it. "Prakash," he said, "if you don't mind, can you please describe to me everything you have seen and heard from the moment you stepped into this house yesterday? Don't leave out any detail, however insignificant it may seem to you at present."

"But, I have already answered all the questions that the police asked me."

"Precisely," he said with a smile. "You see, you answered all the questions *they* asked you. But they didn't let *you* tell them everything. Do you see how incomplete such an exercise can be? They have asked you questions only around those things that *they* have considered important. In fact, in my opinion, they have discovered very little from that interrogation. No, what I would like to do is to let *you* tell me everything."

What Janardan Maity said made sense to me. I took a minute or so and tried to gather my thoughts. Then I described everything in as much detail as possible—right from the moment Arun Mitra welcomed me into the house, till I discovered Mr. Mukherjee's body and returned to the main hall. I didn't leave out any conversation, or anything that I had seen or heard. I also told him about the letter which Mr. Mukherjee had sent me.

Janardan Maity listened with rapt attention, asking one or two occasional questions here and there and seeking clarifications on a few points. After I had finished, he shut his eyes and seemed to think for some time. Then he asked a very curious question: "Tell me one more thing, Prakash. You said Mrs. Nandita Chaudhuri had gone into your uncle's study to make a phone call."

"Yes, she said she was supposed to get back to the city last night itself but she couldn't because of the weather."

"How long was she in the study?" asked Janardan Maity.

I tried to remember. "Must have been around five minutes."

"And where was Anita Mukherjee during those five minutes?"

"She was sitting with me."

"What about Raja? Where was he?"

"He was speaking to Preeti."

"I see. I have one final question, and this is about Anita's murder. I want you to relax and think very carefully before you answer this question."

"All right," I said.

"Very well. When you had walked up to your aunt's body in the corridor last evening, did you notice her right arm?"

I found the question exceedingly strange. I couldn't make head or tail of it. "What do you mean?"

Janardan Maity repeated calmly, "Did you or did you not notice her right arm?"

"I . . . I don't know. I think I did. But what was there to notice?"

"A-ha! Exactly my point!" said Janardan Maity, as his eyes twinkled and his face brightened up.

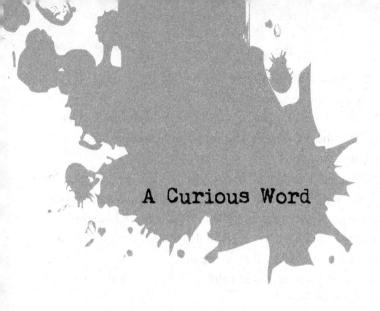

A Curious Word

Janardan Maity left soon after, requesting me to come downstairs after some time. I sat in my room and continued to think of what his strange questions meant. When I had first met him, he had seemed quite eccentric and crazy to me, but I remembered what my uncle had said—he had never won a game of chess with Janardan Maity. Obviously, he could not be crazy. Eccentric, perhaps, but definitely not crazy. The man was obviously thinking in a certain direction. But I could not understand head or tail of it. I came down after sometime and found everyone gathered in the main hall. The storm had stopped, but it was still drizzling outside. A dark gloomy feeling descended upon me as I saw the birthday presents stacked up from the previous night in one corner of the room.

"Three constables have been posted at various places in the house, and Inspector Sanyal will be here later today," announced Janardan Maity.

The events of the previous night were fresh in everyone's mind. As Devendra Mukherjee had predicted, Animesh Sen was seen nursing a black eye. My own fate was hanging on a thin line. Narendra looked as if a hurricane had passed over him. When I saw him in the morning light, it seemed to me that although he may have killed his stepmother in a fit of rage, the grief on his face was genuine, and that in reality, he loved his father and couldn't possibly have murdered him. Nandita Chaudhuri had seemed quite shaken last night, but this morning she had resumed her controlled self. She carried herself upright, as straight as an arrow, and spoke briefly and only when absolutely necessary. Arun Mitra was still gloomy. His sorrow didn't seem to be one bit lesser than that of Narendra. It seemed as if he had lost his own parents. Devendra Mukherjee had played a leading role in bringing much needed order to the house last night, but after his brother was found dead, even he had received a terrible jolt and had become more reticent than ever.

The most surprising change in behaviour was in Preeti. She had completely stopped talking. Her eyes bore evidence to the fact that she had wept all night. Mrs. Mukherjee hadn't seemed to be very comfortable with the way she was hobnobbing with Mr. Mukherjee. Animesh Sen had warned me about her too. I looked at her and wondered if she really had been in a relationship with Rajendra Mukherjee.

Janardan Maity called me and asked me to stay by his side. He walked up to Narendra and I followed him. We sat in front of him, and Janardan Maity said in a soft voice, "Narendra, I'm really sorry for your loss. But I need to ask you something."

Narendra turned towards him and stared at him without saying anything.

Janardan Maity paused for a few moments and then said, "When your . . . when Anita came into your room last night, were you awake?"

For almost a minute or so, Narendra didn't respond. But Janardan Maity stared back at him and waited patiently, politely demanding an answer, without actually uttering a single word. Finally, Narendra said, "She came in. I didn't see her. But I think I heard her voice, I'm not quite sure. I think she called out my name, and said that she had brought dinner."

"What did you say?"

"Nothing."

"Nothing?"

"Nothing. I was . . . I was drunk. And moreover, we hardly . . . talked. We couldn't stand each other."

"Hmm," Janardan Maity responded. "What happened after that?"

"I don't know . . . She left, I guess, and then . . . and then . . ."

"Yes?"

"I heard a noise outside my door; it woke me up. I was in a stupor; wasn't sure what I had heard. My head was aching and then, after sometime—"

"We barged into your room?"

"Yes."

"Hmmm," Janardan Maity knit his brows and seemed to be lost in deep thought. I myself wasn't so sure that Narendra was telling the truth. If he hadn't killed Mrs. Mukherjee, who else could have? Everyone else was in the main hall when I had seen her go into Narendra's room.

Suddenly, like a flash of lightning, I remembered something. I told Janardan Maity that I wanted to speak to him in private. He thanked Narendra and excused himself. I pulled him aside and we found a suitable spot near the study where no one was around.

"Do you realize that there was one person who was *not* in the hall when my aunt's body was found?" I asked him in an excited tone.

"You mean Narendra?"

"No, someone else!"

Janardan Maity frowned curiously and asked, "Who are you referring to?"

"Why? Arun Mitra!"

Janardan Maity looked at me for some time with a faint smile on his lips. Finally, he said, "My dear friend, if you are suggesting that Arun may have lied about finding Mrs. Mukherjee murdered and that, in fact, it was he who was the murderer, then may I remind you that there is a similar allegation against you that's doing the rounds?"

I stammered, and realized that what he was saying was quite true. I wasn't thinking straight. I pinched my forehead in frustration. Janardan Maity patted my shoulders. "Come now, don't kill yourself over it. We ought to get some fresh air."

He walked towards the main door and I accompanied him. We stepped out into the veranda. It was quite cold outside, but the fresh morning air seemed to bring a sense of calm in me. I closed my eyes for some time and felt the cool air on my face. It helped me steady my thoughts.

"Are you all right?" he asked me.

"Yes."

He didn't say anything else for some time. We stood there and looked around. There was a constable sitting on a bench at a distance on the veranda, trying to tear a packet of paan-masala with his teeth. It was still raining, although compared to last night the intensity was much lower. The storm had been a severe one, as was evident from all the broken branches and twigs that were strewn all around. In one corner of the compound, I even saw a corrugated sheet of tin. It was obvious that it had flown off the roof of the cowshed during the storm last night.

Janardan Maity scratched his chin and said, "There was something you said to me this morning which I thought seemed pretty curious."

I looked at him and waited for him to tell me exactly what he was referring to.

"It was just a single word, and it was something that one of the people in the house had told you. So, you see, I am not sure if that was *exactly* what was told to you, or if there was anything lost in communication. But it seemed very significant to me."

I stared back at him. I didn't understand what he was talking about.

He smiled and said, "Let me make it clear for you. You said you had a conversation with your aunt Anita last evening, didn't you?"

"Yes, I did."

And she told you, did she not, that Nandita Chaudhuri had to sell the house after her husband's death?"

"Yes," I said. "But I don't see what is so curious about that."

"Well, death, yes, death . . . Death, but death due to what?" Janardan Maity muttered, as if something was bothering him.

"Why cancer, of course."

"How do you know?"

I now saw what the confusion was all about. "Well, I was

98

having a chat with Mrs. Nandita Chaudhuri earlier last evening, and she told me that her husband had been diagnosed with cancer."

Janardan Maity stared at me with a spark burning in his eyes. "My dear friend, if what you said to me this morning was correct to the verbatim, then I believe your aunt told you that Mrs. Chaudhuri had to sell the house after the *accident*. Don't you find that curious? What accident was she referring to?"

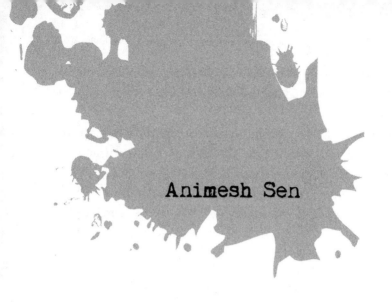

Animesh Sen

I was still trying to fathom what Janardan Maity was trying to indicate. I thought about the entire thing and made my protest: "She may have referred to his death. Surely, that's quite possible?"

Janardan Maity shook his head. "Possible, but unlikely. In fact, highly unlikely. No one refers to a death by a terminal disease as an 'accident'."

I thought for a moment but wasn't convinced. "How can you be sure?"

"Well, there was only one way to find out. To ask the lady who had uttered those words. But, then, the poor woman is dead."

I saw the difficulty, but another solution came to my mind, and I presented it to him. "We can always ask Mrs. Chaudhuri herself, can't we?"

Janardan Maity frowned deeply and sighed. "We can, but it's not going to be so easy. Especially, if . . ."

"If . . .?"

Janardan Maity stared into the void with knit brows for some time. He seemed to be submerged deep within his thoughts. Finally, he nodded his head, as if to shake those very thoughts off his head, and said, "Nothing, it's just a little theory of mine, but its time has not yet come."

We stood in silence as the chilly wind blew all around us. I realized that something about Nandita Chaudhuri was bothering Janardan Maity, but I wasn't quite sure what it might be. Why was he focusing on that one word? Frankly, he seemed to be finding mysteries where there weren't any. I presumed, though, that his intentions were honest. I felt I should do something to put his mind at ease, because even now the frown on his face hadn't disappeared, and he was perching himself up on his toes every now and then, indicating a heightened sense of restlessness. Clearly, I didn't see what harm we could possibly cause if we would ask Mrs. Chaudhuri—in a sensitive manner, of course—what the cause of her husband's death was. And then, a new idea occurred in my mind. What did the death of Nandita Chaudhuri's husband, a tragedy that had happened around five years ago, have to do with the two murders that were committed in the bungalow last night? What possible bearing could it have on yesterday's events?

"So," I said, "are we going to ask Mrs. Chaudhuri about this or not?"

"What do you think?"

"I think we should."

Janardan Maity nodded decisively. "Very well, we will."

Just then the front door opened and Animesh Sen stepped out. He saw us, looked away, and lit a cigarette. I had no intention of coming face to face with him either. Wasn't this the man who had implied just a few hours ago that I had murdered my uncle? What a wretched, miserable man, to even suggest such an idea! I looked away from him in disgust. But I was surprised to see that Janardan Maity called out to him.

"Can I borrow a smoke?" I heard him ask.

Animesh Sen gave both of us a cold look for a few moments, but the smile on Janardan Maity's face lingered on. Finally, he walked towards us and pulled out a pack of cigarettes from his pocket. He gave one to Janardan Maity, and proceeded to bring out his lighter.

"No, I have my matches, thank you," said Janardan Maity, and put his hand in his pocket. "Who do you think is behind all this?"

The question was asked so suddenly and so unceremoniously that it startled Animesh Sen. The discomfort was clearly visible on his face. "My guess is as good as yours," he said briefly.

"Oh no," said Janardan Maity, "you are a lawyer after all. You have the experience in such matters. I'm sure you have a very clear and logical reason to guess who the murderer could be, and I am very interested to know your thoughts on the matter."

Once again Animesh Sen found Janardan Maity staring at his face expecting a response, and it seemed to make him feel quite uncomfortable. He cast one more cold and angry look at him and said in a dismissive manner, "I'm a *civil* lawyer."

"Ah yes! By all means, by all means, I'm sure you are. In fact, we are all civil people here, except the murderer, of course."

Animesh Sen could not bear the sarcasm any longer and took a couple of menacing steps towards Janardan Maity. He gnashed his teeth and said in a gruff tone, "Listen here, both of you. I don't have to guess, you understand? Because I *know* who the murderer is."

Janardan Maity didn't seem to lose his composure one bit. Even his eyes were smiling now. "That's brilliant!" he said. "Would you like to enlighten us?"

"Yeah, why not? I'm not afraid of telling the truth. It's that pretty-face girl. She is the one who killed Mr. and Mrs. Mukherjee."

I was quite surprised. Last night, this man was accusing Narendra and me, and this morning he was accusing someone else! What gall!

"I'm assuming you are referring to Ms. Preeti?" Janardan Maity inquired in a polite manner.

"Yes, who else?" growled the lawyer.

"I think you have something there, you know. And you think the motive could be . . . what? Love, perhaps? A crime of passion?" Janardan Maity asked in all innocence.

"Love, jealousy, *and* money, Mr. Maity. Good old money."

"Yes, I was coming to that. But one thing you simply have to admit—she is exceedingly clever, don't you think?"

Animesh Sen face turned red and he grimaced. "Oh, you bet she is. Shrewd as a viper. Also, she most definitely is a gold-digger. She meets a rich old man and realizes that she will be able to get rich herself in a hurry. In fact, she did not like Mrs. Mukherjee at all. Although she didn't let it show, but I *knew*. There is at least one other person who will corroborate the fact that Preeti was flirting around with Mr. Mukherjee and that she wanted to get his wife out of the way. She figured if she could somehow get rid of that old cow, there was a very good chance that the romantic artist would find solace in her arms instead. And that's all she wanted: to marry him, for his money."

I realized now what Animesh Sen was trying to tell me last night when we had stepped out into the veranda.

Janardan Maity said politely, "I think you have a point. But then, I wonder *how* she could have murdered them, though? Wasn't she in the main hall with all of us when . . ."

Animesh Sen interrupted rashly, "No, she wasn't."

I was shocked to hear such a claim. I looked at Janardan Maity. He was still looking straight at Animesh Sen and listening patiently. The smile on his face hadn't wavered one bit. Animesh Sen went on. "Prakash and I were having a chat. A few minutes later, you and Mr. Mukherjee came and joined us, remember? It was then that I noticed Preeti walking into the dining room, for what reason I have no idea. A few minutes earlier, Anita Mukherjee had walked into the dining room too."

I could not help but interject here. "But Arun Mitra said that Preeti was with him in the hall."

"Rubbish! Utter nonsense. He's lying," Animesh Sen raised his voice by several scales.

Janardan Maity quickly said, "Yes, of course, I agree with you. He's lying. But *why*?"

"What?" Animesh Sen asked in an irritated voice.

"Why would Arun Mitra say that Preeti was with him in the hall, when, as you pointed out, she wasn't?"

Animesh Sen threw away the cigarette stub into the rain and lit another one. "I don't know about that. You should ask him."

Janardan Maity's face was still calm, and his eyes had not moved an inch from Animesh Sen's face. He said, "That I will, Mr. Sen, rest assured . . . that I will."

Then there was a long silence, and Janardan Maity continued to watch Animesh Sen closely. Finally, after almost a minute, Animesh Sen took a couple of puffs and almost in a bid to break the uncomfortable silence, he looked at me and said, "I . . . I'm sorry to have suspected you last night. Clearly, you are not capable of committing a murder."

I didn't know what to say, but Janardan Maity turned to me, let out a laugh, and said, "Hah! I'm not sure if Prakash is feeling relieved or offended by your statement, but please enlighten me on one more thing Mr. Sen, and I assure you, I'll be out of your hair after this. You see, I'm still a little fuzzy on one point. How do you think Preeti committed the second murder? That of Mukherjee's?"

"I don't know that, at least I can't be sure. My theory is that he was stabbed much earlier, soon after he was put to sleep. Preeti was in the room, remember?"

I was about to interject again, but a quick tap on my feet from Janardan Maity's shoes made me realize that he wanted me to keep my mouth shut.

"Yes, I do remember that," said Janardan Maity quickly, "so that's how she achieved her objective of getting rid of both the hurdles on her way."

"Exactly," Animesh Sen said sharply and conclusively.

Janardan Maity stared at his face for some more time. Finally, he extended his hand towards him and said, "Well, you have really helped me get my thinking straight, Mr. Sen. Thank you for your valuable help."

Animesh Sen looked at his hand suspiciously, but shook it, saying "I hope she gets punished for what she has done, that . . . that wretched woman!"

With these final words, he strutted back into the house, leaving us in the veranda.

"Preeti had left my uncle's bedroom much earlier," I said excitedly, immediately after the door had shut behind Animesh Sen. "It was Mrs. Chaudhuri who . . ."

"I know, I know," Janardan Maity raised a hand, and said in an assuring tone.

"You don't understand, she couldn't have killed him. And what good was he to her, if he was dead? If her objective was to get his money, she would never have—"

"So," Janardan Maity interrupted me, "you are saying she lacked *both* motive and opportunity?"

"Absolutely."

"By that logic, are you saying she could have killed your aunt?"

I thought for a moment or two. It did seem possible, now that I thought about it, because she had both motive and opportunity to commit the first murder. Because, as for me, I had not *seen* Preeti in the main hall before Mrs. Mukherjee's body was discovered. I quite liked Arun Mitra and so I had trusted whatever he'd said. Moreover, since everyone was there, chatting and laughing, I had assumed that she was there too. I realized that the problem wasn't as straightforward as I had previously thought. I wasn't sure anymore as to who was lying and who was telling the truth.

"Was Arun Mitra lying when he said Preeti was with him in the main hall?" I asked Janardan Maity.

"Yes!" said Janardan Maity.

"What! But . . . but . . . how can you be so sure?"

"Because I saw her walk into the dining room. Arun did lie."

"But why?" I asked in a shocked voice.

Janardan Maity flashed me an enigmatic smile. "Patience, my friend, patience."

Things were getting all jumbled up in my head once again. The truth was changing by the minute. Fresh facts were coming out in the open every now and then and upsetting the order that I was seeking in my own mind. I remembered I had suspected Arun Mitra, but had quickly dismissed the idea. Now it seemed, he was not such an honest person, after all.

Janardan Maity's voice interrupted my thoughts. "What do you think about our lawyer friend?"

I considered the question for some time before answering it. I did realize that since the first time I met Animesh Sen at the dining table, through the various meetings with him and the various incidents of last evening, his impression on my mind had gone through several changes. But one thing had always stood out—I had never thought of him as the murderer. Now, as I stood in the veranda, mulling Janardan Maity's question in my mind, I wondered why. Animesh Sen was my uncle's legal counsellor. He had a thorough knowledge about his financial affairs. He would also know if my uncle had made any will. One mustn't also forget that Animesh's father was my uncle's close friend. In fact, my uncle was indebted to him. Could it not be possible that Rajendra Mukherjee, in a bid to fill the void created by his own son, and in order to pay his debts to his old friend who had once sheltered him, made provisions for Animesh Sen in his will? And that empowered with the full knowledge of such provisions, Animesh Sen had murdered him? Having done so, was it not possible, in fact natural, that he would try to shift the suspicion from himself to the most likely candidate? Suddenly, I could see why he was so hell bent on accusing others of the murders, first Narendra, then myself, and now Preeti.

"Well, he seems quite cunning to me, that one." I finally answered Janardan Maity's question.

He looked at me and said, "You think so?"

"Yes."

"Why do you say so?"

I hesitated, and then said, "Well, for one, he has been trying to implicate Preeti into the affair since even before the murders took place."

"I think you are referring to the warnings—premonitions, if you will—that she was giving you at this very spot last evening."

"Yes, and later too, at the party."

Janardan Maity was silent for a moment or two. After some time, he said, "Why then, I wonder, would he try to accuse Narendra? Why . . . you know . . . *complicate* things?"

"What do you mean?"

Janardan Maity turned to me and said, "Well, as you said, he had been trying to convince you that Mukherjee's life was in danger, and that the danger was to come from Preeti. He had been doing that all throughout last evening, isn't that right?"

"Well," I paused for a couple of moments, "he didn't actually take names."

"A-ha, exactly! You assumed that he was speaking about Preeti last evening, and the plausibility of your assumption was reinforced by the fact that he took Ms. Preeti's name this morning. Am I not right?"

"Y-yes, I suppose so."

"Fine, now tell me, if he *really* wanted to implicate Preeti in the matter, then he had the most perfect opportunity to do so after Anita's murder, didn't he?"

"What do you mean?" I was perplexed.

"Let's think about it once again, shall we? For some reason, Animesh Sen wants to implicate Preeti, correct?"

"Correct."

"Good, now, just before Anita is murdered, he sees Preeti leave the hall and walk in to the dining room, and minutes before that, Anita Mukherjee has gone into the dining room as well, correct?"

"Correct."

"Excellent. So, why did he accuse Narendra last night, instead of accusing Preeti? Do you think he faked it?"

"No . . . No, I don't think so."

"You are right. In fact, I am convinced that he didn't. He continued to grumble about Narendra even after he had knocked the hell out of him, remember? No, *at that point of time*, he was convinced of Narendra's guilt."

I was quite puzzled. "In that case, why did he accuse Preeti today?"

Janardan Maity frowned. "Why, indeed? Well, I can think of two possible reasons for his having done so. And I think I am right . . . yes, I must be right, there is no other explanation."

"What reasons?" I asked.

"First, our friend is quite unsure of himself. He contradicts himself, left, right, and centre—a trait which is quite un-lawyerlike. I am convinced that he is not having a good trade, that man. Which means he may possibly be in dire straits and in need of money."

"I think I agree. And what's the second reason?" I asked.

"Well, the second reason. Quite possibly the more important of the two reasons. It is that our friend is extremely frustrated."

It seemed quite obvious to me, given his behaviour. "Well, isn't that quite natural? I mean the man possesses certain personality traits which are detrimental to the smooth and successful conduct of his profession. I am not the least bit surprised that he is frustrated!"

Janardan Maity kept looking at me for a long time with a smile on his face. Finally, he said, "You don't see, do you?"

I stammered. "I . . . wha-what do you mean? What don't I see?"

He continued to stare at me for a few more seconds, nodded his head and said, "Nothing. Come, I think we should get back inside the house."

He was fidgeting with the cigarette in his hand, the one he had borrowed from Animesh Sen. I noticed that he had not lit it yet. He saw me looking at it and said, "Do you want this cigarette?"

"No, I don't smoke."

As he threw the cigarette out in the rain and began walking towards the main door, I heard Janardan Maity mutter under his breath, "Nor do I."

Revenge

Janardan Maity and I walked back into the house. There was no one in the main hall, but for a constable standing in one corner. The guests were scattered in various places, some of them upstairs in their rooms. Janardan Maity walked towards the constable and said something. I sat down on a couch, feeling quite exhausted, but with some relief. It seemed to me that there were at least a few people in the house who did not suspect me of having committed the heinous crimes. I looked around the hall. This was where we all were when the two murders were discovered. I had thought that everyone other than Narendra had an alibi, and now I was quite baffled to know that Preeti was not in the room too. Could she have stabbed Mrs. Mukherjee and then entered Narendra's room and planted the dagger under his bed? I couldn't say; I wasn't sure. Somehow, my heart didn't want to believe she could have done it.

In any case, I thought, she could not have committed the second murder. Why would she? If what Animesh Sen said was correct, then she would never want Mr. Mukherjee dead, at least not till *after* he had married her. Moreover, she did not have any opportunity to kill him. I myself left my uncle's bedroom after her, and when I left, he was just fine and fast asleep. Nandita Chaudhuri had gone back to switch off the light, but she was out in an instant. From that point onwards, till the time I walked back into the bedroom, everyone had been in the main hall. In other words, everyone had an alibi, everyone including Narendra.

Suddenly a new thought cropped up in my head. Could it be possible that there was a stranger in the house last night? Someone who had been hiding all the while? Perhaps he waited for an opportunity to sneak away into the night after having committed both the crimes? We never actually thought of searching the house, and it was a big house. I had seen only a part of it. He could have been hiding anywhere. I wanted to share my thoughts with Janardan Maity, but I couldn't find him in the hall. He must have gone up to his room, I thought. Just then I saw Devendra Mukherjee walk into the main hall and I went up to him.

"May I have a word with you please?" I said.

"Sure, tell me?"

I hesitated for a few moments and looked at the constable out of the corner of my eyes. Devendra Mukherjee must have noticed that. "Come, we will sit at the table," he said.

We went to the dining table and sat down. Devendra Mukherjee poured me a glass of water.

"I haven't had a chance to speak to you this morning, are you all right?" he asked.

"Yes, yes. Just that I have never been accused of murder before," I candidly replied with a sheepish grin.

He made a dismissive gesture with his hand and said, "That's utter rubbish! You just came into the house yesterday, why on earth would you want to commit a murder; two, in fact?"

I smiled in relief. "I was wondering . . . do you think it is possible for someone to have come into the house and . . . you know . . . hide somewhere and . . ."

Devendra Mukherjee looked at me keenly for a few moments. "You're saying someone from outside could have broken in?"

"Broken in, or sneaked in. Or perhaps . . ."

"Yes?" he asked, as I hesitated to finish my words.

I didn't want to suggest the third possibility in as many words, but I hadn't forgotten that the doors were all locked from the inside.

The frown on Devendra Mukherjee's face was soon replaced by an expression of comprehension. "I think I see what you are hinting at," he said. "You are suggesting that someone in the house *let* the murderer in?"

"Well . . ." I hesitated again. I wasn't sure how he would take it, because I realized that it would mean suspecting him as well, among other people.

But I was relieved to see that he didn't dismiss my idea altogether and went on to argue objectively. "That's a possibility; there is no doubt about that. One of us could have let the assailant in, and hidden him somewhere. There are plenty of rooms in the house. Then, when we were all in the main hall, he could have come out and committed both the murders, one after the other. Having finished his task, he could then have opened the back door and disappeared into the night. And the person who was aiding him could have simply locked the door once again. It's possible. But . . ."

I could not understand why he was hesitating, so I said, "But you do not think that's what happened?"

Devendra Mukherjee smiled and said, "Well you see, there are several reasons why I don't think it could have happened that way. For one, the entire thing *sounds* quite dramatic, don't you think?"

I thought for a moment or two and nodded in agreement.

"But I do agree that just because it sounds that way does not mean that it could not have happened. But more importantly, *who* could have done such a thing? I mean, let's think about it logically for a minute. Let us assume that for some reason, someone had a grudge against Raja and Anita. Now, if this person, who let the assailant in, wanted to have them murdered, then why do it in a house full of people? He or she could have done it when one or both of them were alone. Wouldn't that have been easier? Why risk being caught?"

I hadn't considered this aspect. Clearly, what he was saying made sense. I remembered that he was approaching the problem in a very logical way last night. I was quite keen to know what he thought about the entire episode, because I was sure that he had deliberated upon the matter overnight. So I asked him.

"See, it's difficult to say. The police will do their work, and I am sure they will apprehend the perpetrator. But I do know this—Narendra is not a stupid chap. I have known him for a long time. When he came back to India with his mother, I had met them. I must say I found his mental strength very admirable. He may have strayed over to the wrong path, but he has a heart of gold. He may have been drunk last night, but I don't believe that he could have killed Anita. He will definitely not make the mistake of stabbing his stepmother and hiding the weapon below his bed. When the police asked me, I told them the same."

"Is there anyone you suspect?" I asked.

Devendra Mukherjee hesitated and cracked his knuckles restlessly. "I do, but I don't think I should comment, because really, I don't have any facts to back my suspicion up."

"I'm sure if you have thought of someone, then there would be a good reason."

Devendra Mukherjee smiled and said, "You trust people too quickly."

I was a little abashed and embarrassed. He went on. "I can't tell you who I suspect. But I will tell you this much, I think the motive here is revenge."

I was quite surprised to hear this, because in my own theories about the tragedy, I had considered a lot of things as the possible motive of the two murders, but revenge had not been one of them. Rajendra Mukherjee was a rich man, and it was natural for one to think that if he was murdered, it would have been for his money. But revenge? I tried to think. If what Devendra Mukherjee was saying was a fact, then my uncle would have committed some kind of a crime, or he would have harmed someone in some way, and someone would have killed him to take revenge. Or, if nothing else, then there was someone who *thought* that my uncle had harmed him or her in some way. I was about to ask Devendra Mukherjee what he meant, when Janardan Maity walked into the dining room.

"There you are!" he said, looking at me.

As he walked up to the table, he greeted Devendra

Mukherjee with a smile and said, "Any word from Inspector Sanyal?"

"I spoke to him earlier today, before he left. He said he would call. I am waiting for that," replied Devendra Mukherjee.

Janardan Maity nodded and said, "He is a very sensible man, the Inspector, don't you think?"

Devendra Mukherjee agreed. "I thought so too. A no-nonsense man, knows his job well, carries a very cool head on his shoulders."

"Did he tell you anything about when we will be allowed to go home?"

"He said he will be visiting later this evening and would speak to all of us in turns. More questioning, I think. Perhaps, after that, we will be excused under the condition that none of us leaves the city."

"Of course, of course," said Janardan Maity with an understanding nod. "Oh, by the way, that black Ford waiting outside with the Red Cross sign on it, I am assuming that's your car?"

"Yes, do you want a drop to the city when we leave?"

Janardan Maity grinned from ear to ear. "You read my mind! Thank you so much! I'm sorry to be a bother, really."

"That's alright, no bother at all. In fact, when I came here yesterday afternoon, I had picked up Anita from her place in the city. I'll drop you, you can come with me. Prakash, do you need a lift too?"

"Yes, that will be very helpful," I said.

"You come here often?" Janardan Maity asked Devendra Mukherjee.

"No," Devendra Mukherjee smiled. "On the contrary, my brother used to complain that I don't give him company.

Actually, you see, Mr. Maity, there was a huge age difference between him and me. Moreover, he had, how shall I say, the finer sensibilities. He loved to talk about art and literature. I don't have much interest in that kind of stuff. So, I ended up not spending much time with him. But now . . ."

An expression of helplessness hovered over Devendra Mukherjee's face. Perhaps he realized that there was nothing he could do to spend time with his brother anymore. He said softly, almost in a murmur, "Now I know I was wrong. I realize now that he had reached an age where there was nothing more valuable to him than the company of his near and dear ones. I failed to see that while Raja was alive."

Janardan Maity sighed and said gently, "How things change . . . over just a few hours, don't they?"

Devendra Mukherjee did not reply. He kept staring at the head of the table, where his brother was seated last evening. Janardan Maity and I looked at each other and decided to leave him alone. We were just about to rise when Devendra Mukherjee rose from his chair and said, "No, it's all right. You folks carry on here. I must get going. I think I will go and see how Narendra is holding up."

After he left, Janardan Maity came and sat next to me and said in a hushed up voice, "I've been looking for you. I have learnt something which you may find quite interesting."

"What is it?" I asked anxiously.

"I was speaking to the constables and they said that the police now think that there was one person who committed both the murders."

"Really?" I exclaimed, "How did they arrive at that conclusion?"

"Shhhh!" Janardan Maity gestured and looked around

him. "Keep your voice down, because the constables told me that they are not really supposed to talk about this."

"I'm sorry," I whispered. "But how can they be so sure that there's only one culprit who committed both the murders?"

"It's just a theory they have, based on the modus operandi. You must have noticed—well perhaps, you weren't in the right frame of mind to notice—but the two daggers were identical."

"Really?"

"Yes, and the police think that quite likely there is just one murderer. You see the police always adopt a certain path in their investigations. Only when they reach a dead end walking on that path do they usually adopt another one."

"I still don't see how—"

"Ah, never mind," Janardan Maity interjected dismissively. "It may not seem logical to you, but you must agree it works heavily in your favour."

I was more baffled. "*My* favour? How come?"

"Don't you see? It exonerates you of the murder of your uncle!"

I stared at him blankly for some time. "Mr. Maity, I am really sorry to have to do this, but I really don't understand what you are talking about."

I was afraid that he would flare up at my stupidity, but Janardan Maity was patience incarnate. He said, "Let me explain. You see you have a water-tight alibi for the murder of Anita Mukherjee, and if the police believe that one person committed both the murders, then there's no way *you* could have killed Rajendra Mukherjee, because at the time of Anita's murder, you were in the main hall, you hadn't moved an inch from there. And there are, let's see, one, two, three, four, five . . . why, there are as many as six people who will vouch for that! So, you did not kill Anita, and therefore you did not kill Raja either."

As the realization sunk in gradually, I was overjoyed and relieved at the same time. Janardan Maity looked at my expressions and smiled at me. "I always knew. It wasn't you," he said.

Although I was very happy to hear that, I asked him, "But *how* did you know?"

"Well," he said, "you are not capable of committing murder."

I smiled and said jokingly, "I don't know whether to feel relieved or offended at that statement!"

Janardan Maity smiled too. "Don't get me wrong. I know you are exceptionally strong on the inside. You demonstrated that last night, when a roomful of strangers accused you of murder and yet you kept your nerves steady. What I meant was that you are not capable of *planning* a murder, or rather, you didn't have the opportunity to do so."

"You think these murders were planned?" I said.

"But of course!" Janardan Maity's said excitedly. "Not just planned, but very carefully planned. Planned to perfection by an exceedingly clever person, a person who had the guts to commit not one, but two murders in a house that was teeming with people. Can you imagine what impeccable planning is required in carrying off a feat like this? And do note, he or she committed the two murders within a very short span of time. Make no mistake, my friend, I am more than certain that this is the work of a person with exceptional intelligence."

"Which is why you believe that Narendra could not have done it? Because he was drunk, right?"

Janardan Maity paused for a moment and said, "Let's just say that he is not at the top of my suspect list."

I was surprised. I said, "You have a *list* of people you suspect?"

"Why, don't you?" Now Janardan Maity seemed shocked.

"I-I mean . . ." I wasn't sure what to say.

"Very well, I am going to ask you a few questions. You'll have something to think about. See if you find answer to these questions, and you'll be closer to the truth."

I sat upright and said, "All right."

"One, what accident was Anita Mukherjee referring to? Two, why did Arun lie about Preeti's alibi? Three, why did Preeti walk into the dining room, minutes after Anita had walked into the same room? And four, who is the person Animesh Sen was referring to when he said that at least one other person will tell us that Preeti was flirting with Raja?"

I must say I didn't have the least amount of idea about any of the answers. But I made a mental note of the questions. Janardan Maity was about to leave, so I told him about my little chat with Devendra Mukherjee.

"I must say I agree with him," he said. "This was the work of one of the guests. No outside party could have been involved."

I quickly asked, "And what he said about revenge?"

Janardan Maity frowned, and muttered under his breath, "That is very interesting . . . what he said there. Revenge . . . revenge . . ."

He seemed lost in his thoughts for quite some time, so much so that several minutes passed by, and he didn't move. I waited for some time, but soon I reached the end of my patience. I called out to him. "Mr. Maity?"

"Hmm?" he seemed to have come out of a stupor. "Oh yes, I'm sorry. I was just . . . an idea . . ."

"You think there was something in what he said?"

"Sorry, there was something in what who said?"

"Devendra Mukherjee?"

"Yes, yes, I think so. I'll thank him when I see him next, because he has opened a new window in my mind. I think it is high time we spoke to Mrs. Chaudhuri."

"Mrs. Chaudhuri?"

"Yes, as soon as possible. Listen, I'm going to make a few calls. And then I intend to speak to Nandita Chaudhuri. Would you like to be a part of that discussion?"

"Oh yes, most definitely," I said. The mystery was becoming deeper and deeper, and I didn't want to be a mere bystander.

"Excellent, in that case, I'll meet you in the main hall in about half an hour."

Janardan Maity left, almost in a hurry. I walked out of the dining room and went back to the main hall. The lone constable was still sitting there, but no one else was to be seen.

I found Mahadev in the kitchen and asked him if he had seen Mrs. Chaudhuri. He said she would probably be in her room. Her room was apparently on the ground floor itself, near Arun Mitra's room. Mahadev asked me if I was hungry. The fact was that I was starving, and I told him so. He turned around a quick sandwich for me, which I consumed heartily.

I met Janardan Maity in the main hall and I told him that Nandita Chaudhuri could be found in her room. Soon, we knocked on her door and asked her if we could have a word with her. She welcomed us in and we sat down on a couple of chairs. Nandita Chaudhuri sat on her bed and looked at us inquisitively.

"Mrs. Chaudhuri," Janardan Maity began in a respectful

manner, "please excuse me for having to bother you under these circumstances. But, it is of utmost importance that I ask you a few questions."

Nandita Chaudhuri looked at our faces one after the other, and then said strongly, "Is this some sort of an interrogation? Because, if it is—"

"Oh no, no, no, Mrs. Chaudhuri," Janardan Maity interjected. "I assure you, I wouldn't dream of interrogating you. What authority do I have to do such a thing? No, not at all. I merely want your *help*."

I couldn't help but admire Janardan Maity's tact, because Nandita Chaudhuri's voice softened immediately. "How can I help you, Mr. Maity?" she asked.

Janardan Maity didn't say anything immediately. I stole a glance at him to realize that he was choosing his words carefully. After a few moments he said, "Mrs. Chaudhuri, I know this must be difficult for you. But please, I implore you to bear with me, and answer just *one* question of mine."

"Which is?" Nandita Chaudhuri asked calmly.

Janardan Maity stared at her intently for some time and said, "How did your daughter die?"

The Accident

The question was so unexpected, so sudden, and so brutal, that I felt my legs tremble under me. I could only wonder what the poor woman, sitting on the bed, would have gone through. I was extremely upset with Janardan Maity for having asked such a question. It was quite evident from Nandita Chaudhuri's face that her feelings matched mine. She frowned in great dissatisfaction and said in a cold, steely voice, "Mr. Maity, what nonsense are you talking about!"

Janardan Maity didn't move. He kept staring at her.

Mrs. Chaudhuri said, "If this is your idea of a joke, I must tell you that it's in extremely poor taste. Why, you . . . how could you . . . how could you even . . . say something like that?"

It was disgraceful to see that Janardan Maity didn't even flinch. He kept staring at the woman's face, which was now twisted and convulsed in

123

disgust and anger. But Janardan Maity didn't utter a single word.

"How could you?" Mrs. Chaudhuri went on. Her entire form had shrunk, trying to get away as far from Janardan Maity as possible. The colour on her face had turned red and she continued to ask in sheer disgust, "How could you? How could you? How can anyone . . .?"

I felt so sorry for the poor woman that I instantly decided to take Janardan Maity away and out of the room and leave her alone. I wondered what had gotten into him to ask such a nasty question to such a nice and polite woman. It was most disturbing. Wanting to take a strong stance in the matter, I took a step towards Janardan Maity and said in a stern voice, "Now, look here, Mr. Maity," when I saw Nandita Chaudhuri bury her face in her palms, only to start sobbing bitterly.

Janardan Maity still didn't move or say a word. It seemed to me he had turned into a statue of stone. I felt so repulsed by the man that I felt like holding him by the scruff of his neck and throwing him out of the room.

And then I heard the muffled words of the poor woman, accompanied with uncontrollable spasms of sobbing. "She was so beautiful . . . so beautiful . . . *so beautiful.*"

I looked at the woman in sheer shock, and then at Janardan Maity, who had a strange expression on his face. In it I saw, for the first time, an expression of victory, which slowly gave way to a look of genuine sympathy. He looked at me and made a gesture towards the corner of the room. I followed his gaze and realized what he wanted me to do. I poured a glass of water and brought it to the weeping woman.

Janardan Maity put a soft hand on her shoulder and said,

"Madam, I have met a lot of brave people in my life, but never have I met someone as brave as *you*."

I could do nothing but wait, because everything was shrouded in the dense fog of mystery. Janardan Maity took the glass of water from my hand and said in a soft voice, "Come now, madam, calm down. Have some water."

When Mrs. Chaudhuri controlled herself and pulled her face up from her palms, I felt really sorry for her. I remembered having seen her little face and frame at the table last evening and having wondered how dignified and resolute she looked. Where was that face now? Where had it gone? I saw a miserably weak and crestfallen little woman trembling all over even as she tried to control her tears. Her nose was runny and her face had turned crimson. She could not even look straight at us. I felt really, really bad for her.

As Janardan Maity tried to calm her down, my mind, which was now deeply unsettled, coughed up a memory from last night. I remember having heard that Nandita Chaudhuri had a daughter, but till a few minutes ago I had believed her to be alive and well. Why, I had even assumed it was her daughter that she had called last evening to say that she would not be coming home. What was going on? My heart was beating so loud, I could feel the thumps at the back of my head. Meanwhile, having settled down a bit, Nandita Chaudhuri began to speak.

"My husband and I had been married for twelve years, Mr. Maity. Twelve long yet happy years. Happy, because there was no other man like him; soft-spoken, honest, gentle, considerate, well-mannered. He made me smile, and told me every day that everything would be all right. But no matter how hard we prayed, no matter what promises I made to the almighty, no matter how much I begged, I couldn't bear a child. We had everything. Everything. But yet, we had nothing. Except each other. I leant on him, and he on me. And we kept walking. We built this house with all our savings, and we started to live amidst nature. We would take long walks into the woods and he would make me smile. We kept walking. Not even once did he let me know that somewhere deep within him, a monstrous wound was growing, one that was devouring him inch by inch. He knew I was sad, and perhaps he knew that he could not afford to break one more bad news to me. So, like the angel he was, he kept it to himself. And foolish as I was, I continued to pity myself, and didn't even notice that he was withering away. His health was failing right in front of my eyes, but difficult as it may be for anyone to believe, I simply didn't notice. I'll never forgive myself for that."

Nandita Chaudhuri paused for a moment. I had not moved a muscle, and neither had Janardan Maity. He was calm and kept staring at Mrs. Chaudhuri's face.

"And then, there was a miracle," Nandita Chaudhuri's face beamed as she continued. "A little angel came into my womb. My precious, precious little girl was born. Naturally, I was happy. But my husband? He was *ecstatic*! He was jumping around in joy, hugging strangers on the road. You should have seen him! I now know why. He was happy because he had realized that after he was gone, I would not be left all alone. That I would have a purpose in my life."

"As a new mother, I was happy, but my happiness was short-lived. For my husband's cancer was now beyond hiding. We tried our best. But it was too late. Within a year of the birth of our daughter, my husband passed away. God seemed to have made a cruel bargain with me. He gave me my daughter and took away my husband. Moreover, without paying any heed to his protests, I had spent a significant amount of money in trying to save him. And in doing so, I had borrowed a lot of money from friends and relatives. After the initial words of consolation and encouragement, almost all of them demanded their money back. I didn't have any money left. But I did not give up. I started teaching in a school in the city. I put the house on rent, and I myself lived in this very room with my daughter. The Mukherjees were the tenants. Eventually, I was able to pay off my debts. I was raising my daughter well. As my husband had thought, she was the sole purpose that I continued to pin my hopes on. And then, the incident happened."

Mrs. Chaudhuri's hands suddenly trembled and a look of terror came on her face.

"There was a piano, on the first floor landing. It had been with the Mukherjees since their London days, and it was the kind that had wheels on its legs. Mishti was playing with her doll at the foot of the stairs on the ground floor. Narendra had come visiting—as he often used to when he was broke. He was drunk, as was Mr. Mukherjee. An argument ensued, and it quickly turned into a nasty quarrel. Narendra accused his father of leaving his mother to rot and die. Mr. Mukherjee was insanely enraged on hearing this and he hit his son across the face. Narendra tumbled onto the piano. Its wheels had not been locked in. It rolled across the landing and . . . fell . . . fell . . . down the . . . down the . . . down the stairs."

My legs were trembling so much that it was becoming difficult for me to remain standing. Janardan Maity's jaws had hardened too.

"I was there, Mr. Maity. I saw it all," sobbed Nandita Chaudhuri, with a horrified expression on her face. "Have you ever heard a piano roll down a flight of stairs, Mr. Maity? Oh, that sound . . . that horrid, *horrid* sound. As if the devil himself, yes . . . the devil himself was descending down the stairs! And then . . . and then . . . with a l-loud crash . . . I-I c-couldn't . . . I couldn't do *anything*. I was right there, Mr. Maity, but I couldn't do anything. It was all over. It was . . ."

With a sudden outburst Mrs. Chaudhuri flung herself on the bed and started wailing. I shall not even endeavour to describe the poor woman, for no words created and understood by man have the ability to describe the mourning of a mother who has witnessed her child's death in front of her eyes.

I Investigate

After around an hour or so, as I was sitting in the main hall, Janardan Maity came and sat beside me, seemingly exhausted. He said Mrs. Chaudhuri had been able to calm herself down and that she was resting.

"It is best to leave her alone at the moment," he said, "because she is the kind of woman who is at her best when she is alone."

We sat there in silence, but my mind was very restless. After sometime I asked Janardan Maity, "How did you know?"

"Hmm?" Janardan Maity seemed to come out of a stupor. His face looked tired, "You mean about the accident?"

"Yes."

"I didn't at first. But when you told me that Devendra Mukherjee had spoken to you about revenge, Anita Mukherjee's reference to the 'accident' made sense to me. So, I called up Inspector

Sanyal and asked him if he was aware of any accidental deaths in this house in the past. He said he wasn't. Then I asked him if, during his interrogation of Mrs. Chaudhuri, he had asked her about the date of her husband's demise. On learning that the house had been sold to Mukherjee more than one year after Mr. Chaudhuri's death, I saw a strong possibility that the 'accident' had nothing to do with Mr. Chaudhuri. The rest was sheer guesswork."

"Guesswork?" I asked in a shocked tone.

"Yes," Janardan Maity replied calmly.

"You asked her such a question about her child, based on a guess?" My voice rose. I was finding it difficult to contain my dissatisfaction.

"Yes, because I have to arrive at the truth."

"What truth? What are you talking about?"

"Well," Janardan Maity shrugged, "we now know that she had a very strong reason to murder your uncle."

On hearing these words, I suddenly found the man extremely despicable.

"How can you suggest something like that? Her daughter *died!* She was crushed to . . . death." I found it difficult to find my words. Unknown to myself, my features must have contorted, and the irritation must have been clearly visible on my face, because Janardan Maity looked at me for some time and remarked, "Emotion is a strange thing, my friend, because it can be a strength as well as a weakness. And make no mistake, I cannot afford to be weak at this critical juncture. I don't care if she had a personal tragedy."

"You don't care?" I asked, exasperated and disgusted.

"No," said Janardan Maity coolly. "You see I am on the lookout for the truth."

"Oh, come on," I snapped, "the truth, the truth. What have you done so far to get *any* closer to the truth than where we were last night, huh?"

My outburst was quite natural. The man was all pomp and show. To hell with him and his logic. I *knew* for a fact that Nandita Chaudhuri couldn't have killed my uncle. I knew it in my guts, and I didn't need logic to back it up. Janardan Maity had no words in response. He simply rose and muttered something vague, like "It's time for me to remain alone for some time."

I didn't care to respond and he walked away. I was still angry and was pacing up and down the hall. I was feeling quite frustrated. It was well past noon, and we were nowhere even remotely close to identifying the killer. And to think that he or she was loitering around the house—that was unpardonable. I quickly made up my mind. I would do my own investigation. I would write down all the facts—everything that I had seen and heard and learnt in the last few hours—in my notebook and revisit them in an orderly fashion, looking for clues and pointers. If necessary, I would ask questions to the suspects, establish motive, question and cross-question alibis. I would find the killer *myself*.

I went up to my room and took out my notebook. I opened a fresh page. For a few moments I gathered my thoughts. I realized it would be best to go by the alibi route and cross-reference that with motive. That would save me a lot of work. So, I wrote down the following:

Facts in the Case of the Murders of Rajendra and Anita Mukherjee		
Suspect	Alibi	Motive
Nandita Chaudhuri	Was with me when Mr. M was last seen alive.	Revenge? (Unlikely suspect) (Does DM know anything about the incident?)
Preeti (surname not known)	No alibi for Mrs. M's murder. Was seen walking into dining room, minutes after Mrs. M had walked into the same room.	Money cannot be the motive. Love? Jealousy?
Arun Mitra	Shaky alibi before Mrs. M's murder (JM says he saw him in the hall—is JM to be trusted?) Also, he discovered the body.	Money could be a big motive, if Mr. M would have made provisions for the secy who was 'like a son' to him.
Narendra Mukherjee	No alibi during Mrs. M's murder. Most likely suspect.	Money. Inheritance. Hatred. (Case against him VERY strong)

Devendra Mukherjee	Was in conversation with Nandita Chaudhuri during Mrs. M's murder.	If he doesn't know about the accident, then why did he refer to 'revenge'? Has he ever been harmed by his elder brother at any time?
Animesh Sen	Was in conversation with me during Mrs. M's murder.	Perhaps money? (But seems quite incapable of planning & committing both the murders. Restless. Shifty.)
Janardan Maity	Was in conversation with me during Mrs. M's murder.	Revenge?

As I went over the table several times after I had finished creating it, I realized a few important points, and like a true detective, I meticulously wrote them down one by one.

1. VERY little is known of Janardan Maity. Who is he? What motive could he have? What was his relationship with Mr. & Mrs. M? Had he ever been harmed by one or both of them?
2. Need to question Arun Mitra. Why did he lie?

3. Need to know more about Mr. M's last will.
4. Does DM know about the accident?

And then, as I read the table more carefully several times, I jotted down a few more points.

5. Can 'Money' really not be the motive for Preeti? What if her name appears on Mr. M's will?
6. Can 'Revenge' be the motive for Animesh Sen? Or Preeti?
7. Isn't Narendra the most likely suspect if we take 'Revenge' as the motive?
8. Isn't Narendra the most likely suspect if we take 'Money' as the motive?

After writing these points, I started feeling a little frustrated myself. Really, what a fine mess it was for Narendra! He had not one but two extremely probable motives, *and* he had no alibi at all. In addition to that, the murder weapon was found right under his bed. That's just amazing; there was no way I could save him.

Then I had a realization. I figured that I *wanted* Narendra to be innocent, just like I *wanted* Nandita Chaudhuri to be innocent. It was then that I realized that what Janardan Maity was doing was in fact right. He was suspecting everybody. Isn't that what any good detective should do? I picked up my pen and wrote a final point—

9. 'Revenge': most likely for Nandita Chaudhuri.

The pen fell out of my hand and rolled across the table. I rubbed my eyes. This was not going anywhere. I went to the bathroom and splashed water on my face. I looked at myself in the mirror. My face looked haggard and my eyes were all bloodshot. I needed a shave too. I came back to the room and drank a glass of water. Then I paced up and down the room for some time. I was getting more and more restless with every passing minute. At one time, I considered going and speaking to Janardan Maity. The man had a nice method, if nothing else. But moments later my ego made me dismiss such a plan. I firmed up my mind and decided to continue my own solo and unaided investigation. I went back to the table and started going over my notes once again. But unfortunately even after an hour or so I did not make any progress.

Soon, sleep came over me and I found myself dozing off repeatedly, in between studying my notes. After some time, although I wasn't exactly sure how much time, I woke up with a jolt. It was right then that I heard footsteps right outside my door. The sound was very faint, almost unnoticeable, and that's exactly why it aroused my curiosity. Because I had heard footsteps outside this room earlier as well, and they had not been so faint. It was then that the realization dawned upon me.

This person was tiptoeing!

Very carefully, I rose from my chair and took off my sandals. Then I myself tiptoed to the door and placed my ear on the wood. There was no mistake. The person was just outside my door. I could hear heavy breathing.

What did he want? Was he trying to come in? A wave of terror engulfed me and I started to shiver. Why would he try to hide his presence? It could mean only one thing—that the person waiting and breathing just outside my door was trying to enter my room. Very slowly, without making any sound, I pulled away from the door. Step, by step, by step, until my back hit the wall behind me. I waited, and then my eyes suddenly fell on the bolt of the door. I cursed and cursed and cursed myself. The door was not bolted from the inside! All that the man had to do was to push it open.

A desperate cry for help found its way upwards from inside me, but by the time it reached my lips, it had died down. I realized that my throat was completely parched, and that I had no strength left in me. I could not shout for help.

I waited for the assailant to barge in and drive a dagger through my heart, as he had done to my uncle and aunt. The moments passed by. The clock on the wall ticked away without a care in the world. I didn't even know that the clock had existed until now.

After sometime, I realized that if I were to open the door suddenly and run outside, I may be able to startle the murderer and tackle him down to the floor, just like in a rugby match. I made up my mind. Like a cornered dog, I bared my teeth, counted to three and made a dash. I opened the door and was about to step outside when I realized that there was no one outside. But . . . what just happened? I could have sworn there was someone standing there just a few moments ago. Where did he go?

I slowly extended my neck outside and looked towards the left. This was the side of the stairs. The passage continued for some distance and turned sharply towards the staircase. Mr. Mukherjee's room was also on this side. The passage was empty. Where did the man go? I looked towards the right. And the instant I did so, I was immediately forced to pull my head back in.

There was someone tiptoeing through the passage. It was a man!

Taking a few moments to gather all my courage, I extended my neck out again like a tortoise, just enough for my eyes to catch a glimpse of the murderer, making sure I was not seen.

Too late! I saw the man again for one fleeting second before he turned around the corner. He was wearing a brown flannel jacket.

I don't know what came over me in the next few seconds. My blood began to boil. I went back to the table and picked up a pair of scissors that was lying on it. I stepped onto the passage barefoot. I ensured that I didn't make my presence known, but I wasn't afraid anymore. This man had killed my uncle and aunt. It was imperative that he be caught. I would catch him and hand him over to the police. I had played hockey in school for four years. It would come in handy today.

I took my steps carefully, without making any sort of sound at all. If the assailant were to know that he was being followed, he would realize that I was on to him and I'd perhaps never be able to catch him again. What's more, he may even decide to turn around and attack me. When I reached the corner, I carefully peeped around it. The man was nowhere to be seen. There was only one door on this side of the house. Clearly, the murderer must have gone in there, because there was nowhere else to go. Whose room was it? I had no idea.

On the far side of the door, there was a window on the wall that opened into the room. I could see it from where I was standing, and it was evident that it had glass panes and that they were shut. Also, they were presently covered with curtains from the inside. I nevertheless decided to go ahead and try to see if I could get a peep inside. Blood was flowing through my veins so fast that it made a rushing sound in my ears. I pursed my lips together and crossed the door very carefully. I was now next to the window, but alas, it was entirely covered with heavy red curtains. I bit my fingers and cursed my luck. I had no other option but to go back downstairs and try to find out who was staying in this room. But then, I noticed that there was a small gap on one side of the window, between the frame and the edge of the curtain.

I put my forehead on the glass and tried to peep through the tiny gap. At first, I couldn't make out anything, but as my eyes focused and adjusted themselves, I saw the murderer inside.

Arun Mitra!

Before the initial shock could subside, I realized that he had grabbed someone from behind by placing his strong arm around the person's neck in a death grip that was sure to squeeze the life out of the victim. I couldn't see who the poor victim was because Arun's back was turned towards me. Unsure of what to do, I hesitated for a few moments. And in those moments, the victim somehow managed to struggle free of Arun's grasp and turned around to face him.

Preeti!

My entire body arched into readiness. I had to do something, and quickly! Otherwise he would kill her. I clutched on to the scissors with all my might and was just about to fling myself onto the door, ready to smash it if necessary, when Preeti lunged forward, threw her arms around Arun's neck and planted a passionate kiss on his lips.

My jaw dropped and my brain shut down. I was not able to process what my eyes were seeing. *Preeti? Arun?* Just then, a sudden tap on my shoulders startled the living daylights out of me and I swung around, ready to strike.

I had raised the scissors above my head, with the intention

of driving it through the chest of the person standing behind me and breathing down my neck. But with a firm push, his hand forced it down. His other hand shot up with the swiftness of a cobra, his index finger hovering over his lips, prohibiting me from making any sound.

After he had pulled me away from the window, turned the corner, thrust me into my room, and shut the door behind him, Janardan Maity smiled and said, "*Now* you know!

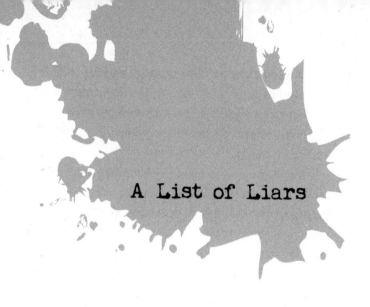

A List of Liars

When I came down for lunch, I was in a daze, so much so that quite a few people at the table asked me if I was feeling okay. I don't remember what I may have said in response. I glanced across the table and looked at Janardan Maity, who seemed to be concentrating on the food at the moment. He had refused to answer any of my questions after my little adventure, ruthlessly leaving me in total darkness. Arun and Preeti sat far from each other, and seemed unusually quiet. I was quite sure that they were aware that their amorous little encounter had been discovered. Nandita Chaudhuri had regained her composure and it was good to see that she was holding her head upright once again. Devendra Mukherjee and Animesh Sen were having a conversation but I couldn't hear what they were saying. Only Narendra was missing from the table.

I could hardly eat. My brain was failing me, as it had done at alarming intervals since the murders, and I was, once again, unable to process so many bits and pieces of information that had been sent to it mercilessly over the last few hours. As one question after another started cropping up in my head, I banished them—religiously and systematically—vowing that I would *not* think about the murders anymore. I would simply wait it out and see what the police did.

After some time, Devendra Mukherjee announced, "Inspector Sanyal called me some time back. He is on his way here. He has asked all of us to . . . er . . . to stay indoors. There's nothing to worry, there are constables all around the house."

His assurances seemed quite futile, as was evident from the expressions on the faces of people around the table. I myself had no hope left. Frankly, from what I had seen since last night, I wouldn't be surprised anymore if everyone around the table would suddenly jump up and start stabbing each other in the heart. And honestly, I couldn't care less. This was all just a bad dream, and I would simply have to wait it out.

After lunch, I immediately proceeded to walk up to my room, but just as I was about to leave, Janardan Maity came up to me and held me by my hand. "I know you are upset with me, Prakash," he muttered under his breath in a low voice, "but all I ask of you is patience."

I looked at him. What a strange man he was, much unlike the first impression that he had created on me during the funny incident with the umbrella. Could he be the murderer? Yes, of course, why not? But I still found myself listening to him.

"Come with me to the study," he went on. "Please?"

A few minutes later, he had made me sit in a cushioned chair in the study, and himself stood in the centre of the room after closing the door behind him. Like the rest of the house, this room too had been done up with love and care. The mahogany table at the centre was majestic, and surrounding it, standing like respectful sentries, were several bookcases. There was not an inch of empty space on the shelves.

"Your mind," Janardan Maity said with a soft smile on his face. "It must be playing tricks on you, isn't it?"

I didn't reply.

He looked at me fondly. "Be patient, my friend. These things are never easy. It is one thing to read about them in detective stories—where the sleuth is of extraordinary intelligence and his assistant is a faithful friend, and they encounter brutal murders and stumble upon one shocking discovery after another, and you read about them, curled up inside your warm blanket, with a cup of coffee in your hand on a rainy night, knowing very well that you yourself are safe. You root for the protagonist, no doubt, but you *aren't* the protagonist. No matter how good the writer's skill, you will never be able to feel the true gravity of the situation because it's not about the death of someone *you* know. But this? No, this is different, Prakash. This is not fiction. This is as real and as heinous as it can get. Murder, it's always such a nasty thing. The taking away of a human life. Death! Gruesome, cruel, ugly, nasty death. And not in the natural order of things, mind you. Death, deliberately brought upon someone who the victim trusted. The horror in their eyes, the shock that remains plastered on their faces in their last moments. No, these are not easy things to experience at all. Nine out of ten people go through their lives not witnessing *any* violent death, let alone murder. And you, my dear friend, you have seen two of them in one night. No wonder your nerves are rattled. It's nothing to be ashamed of."

Having finished his little speech, he came and sat down beside me.

Although I wasn't thinking straight, I must admit that his words had a soothing effect on my nerves. For some reason, and I can't explain why, I wanted to trust him. I turned to him and said, "I need to know."

"No," he said in a calm voice. "You don't. Not now."

"But I do," I protested. "I have so many questions bombarding my head from all directions. I need to find answers."

Janardan Maity looked at me with concern for some time. Then he let out a deep sigh and asked, "Are you sure?"

"Yes, I am sure," I said.

He paused for a few more seconds and then seemed to make up his mind.

"Very well," he said, "what do you want to know?"

I hesitated for a moment, because I wasn't prepared at all. Then, I steadied my nerves and said, "Who killed my uncle and aunt?"

"I don't know," Janardan Maity answered plainly.

"*You don't know?*"

Janardan Maity looked at me keenly and said, "I am not sure what you think of me, Prakash, but . . ."

"I'll tell you what I think of you. You're a detective, aren't you?" I interrupted.

"No!" he shouted, with a frown. "Whatever gave you that idea?"

"But surely you must be . . . I don't mean a police detective, but more like a private investigator?"

Janardan Maity smiled and nodded his head, "You read too much crime fiction and mystery novels, don't you? Sherlock

Holmes . . . Hercule Poirot . . . or our very own Byomkesh Bakshi and Feluda?"

I didn't respond. It was true that I was a die-hard fan of detective stories. Janardan Maity went on. "No, Prakash. I am not a detective of any kind, public or private. I have no special powers. If you are looking for a super-sleuth in me, I must tell you right now, my friend—*don't*. I am an ordinary man."

I wasn't sure whether his statements were being made in genuine modesty, or whether what he was saying was a fact. But I decided to let the matter pass and asked him my next question, "Did you know that Arun and Preeti were . . .?"

"In love? Yes, that I did."

"How did you know?"

Janardan Maity smiled and said, "Those famous detectives I just mentioned, if they would have been real, and if you would have had a chance to ask them, even they would have told you that you don't need to be a detective to find out if a young man and woman are in love with each other. All you need is to keep your eyes and ears open. And mind you, there's at least one more person in this house who knows that Arun and Preeti are in love with each other."

"Really? Who is that?"

"Animesh Sen."

"But . . . how do you know that?"

"Didn't Animesh Sen's behaviour strike you as being distinctively odd?"

"Yes, it did but what's that got to do with . . ."

Janardan Maity raised his hand. "Hang on a second. Don't get ahead of your thoughts. What exactly struck you as odd in his behaviour?"

144

"Well, for one, he seemed quite frustrated and restless," I replied instantly.

"Very good! What else?"

I thought for a few moments, before saying, "He seemed to be hell bent on accusing Preeti."

"Very good! Go on, develop your theory now. I know you can do it."

I was really not sure if his faith in me was misplaced, but I did decide to give it a try. I went over the facts in my mind. I thought about all the characters involved in this side-story. I remembered how Animesh Sen was looking with hateful eyes at my uncle and Preeti when they were chatting with each other at the party last night. And then suddenly, it occurred to me like a flash of lightning!

"Animesh is himself in love with Preeti!" I exclaimed.

"Excellent! Excellent!" Janardan Maity clapped his hands with childlike glee.

"But . . . but—"

"But if he is love with her, why accuse her—is that what you are wondering about?"

"Yes, it seems very unnatural."

Janardan Maity smiled and nodded his head. "Not at all! On the contrary, it is the most natural reaction of a man who is accustomed to having his way every time. He met Preeti. I wouldn't be surprised if Preeti *did* give him the feeling that she was interested in him. It may or may not be intentional, but she does have the habit of doing that, making men feel attracted to her, and giving them the impression that she is approachable, don't you think, Prakash?"

Janardan Maity was looking at me with narrow eyes and a mischievous smile. I flushed. I myself had felt weak in the knees when she had looked at me with her deep, beautiful eyes. Later, throughout the evening, I had tried to steal glances at her. Now I knew that Janardan Maity had noticed everything.

"But imagine Animesh's misery," Janardan Maity went on, "when he finds out that Preeti loves Arun instead. His instant reaction is that of anger—not for Arun, but for Preeti herself, the woman who had 'made him fall in love' with her, and then mercilessly crushed his advances."

"So, did Preeti really kill Mrs. Mukherjee?"

Janardan Maity shut his eyes and shook his head. "As I have told you, I don't know."

"But, we do know that she had followed her into the dining room, don't we?"

"No, we don't. We know that she had gone into the dining room. The two are not the same thing."

"So, we are back to square one?" I said in a frustrated voice.

With a sad smile on his face, Janardan Maity said, "Don't say I didn't warn you. You wanted answers."

"But, have we not made *any* progress so far? In trying to identify the murderer, I mean?" I asked. There must have been a lot of desperation in my voice. Janardan Maity raised his hand in an assuring gesture and said, "I wouldn't go to the extent of saying that we haven't learned anything."

"What have we learnt?" I demanded.

Janardan Maity's eyes narrowed and he looked at me keenly. "Why don't *you* tell me what we have learnt, for a change?"

I considered the facts for some time and decided to share my thoughts with him.

"Well," I began, "one or two people have lied in the past few hours. And—"

"One or two?" interrupted Janardan Maity.

"Yes, I mean, for instance, Arun Mitra lied."

"You mean, when he said that Preeti was with him when Anita was murdered?"

"Yes. And now, well, in the light of the new discovery, it seems quite natural, you know? His having done so."

Janardan Maity said, "Yes, it does. Very good. Go on."

I chose my next words carefully. "If facts were facts, Mrs. Chaudhuri also lied."

Janardan Maity smiled and nodded. I felt a little embarrassed that I had snapped at him sometime back when he had told me that he still suspected Nandita Chaudhuri. But Janardan Maity didn't mention it and nor did I.

I went on. "Despite everything that has happened, I mean with Mrs. Chaudhuri in the past, she did lie that her daughter was alive. *Why?*"

"More importantly, who did she call last night?"

"If she really did make a call at all?" I added. My mind was working again.

"Excellent," Janardan Maity said appreciatively. "Please proceed."

"And then there's Preeti herself."

"What about her?"

"She also lied about her alibi. She actually didn't have one. She was not with Arun in the hall. She was in the dining room."

"I agree. You're doing really well."

I went over things in my mind for a few seconds and said, "That's a list of people who lied. Now, as for the motives and alibis—"

"Hang on a second!" Janardan Maity yelled out at the top of his voice.

I was startled and stopped midway with a sudden jerk.

"Is that all?" Janardan Maity spread out his arms and asked in a grave voice.

"What? What do you mean?" I had no idea what he was talking about.

Janardan Maity said, "I mean do you think these are the only people who have told lies since last evening?"

"Why, yes, of course. I can't think of anyone else."

"But I can," Janardan Maity's voice rose as his eyes sparkled in excitement.

I didn't know what to say. I knew I wasn't a very intelligent man, but I didn't know who else could have lied.

"Well, I am all ears," I said, "although I do think I have covered everyone."

"Oh, but you have forgotten the most important lie of all!" He was so excited that he stood up and spread his arms.

"Which is?" I asked.

"Why, the one that your uncle told!"

I had no idea what he was talking about, so I simply stared blankly at him.

"Don't you remember? At the table, during the introductions. He had said that Nandita Chaudhuri had sold the house and moved to the city with her daughter. That was a lie! A deliberate lie!"

"Yes, yes, but . . ." I said.

"Albeit a lie to shield his son, but still," Janardan Maity bent forward and raised a finger, "a lie!"

I nodded my head slowly and agreed with him. What he was saying was true. "Yes, but what does that have to do with his murder?"

"Everything, don't you see?" Janardan Maity seemed quite

surprised that I couldn't see. He went on. "Picture this. Raja and his son have a quarrel. An accident happens, as a direct outcome of the quarrel. And as an outcome of that accident, a mother witnesses the death of her child. Her sole purpose of living on is crushed in front of her eyes. And what does Raja do? He shields his son. He hushes things up. One parent protects his child, while the other weeps at her child's death."

I protested. "But it was an accident."

"Explain that to *her*!" Janardan Maity said coldly.

I hung my head. I agreed with every word that Janardan Maity had said. No matter how much my uncle would have consoled her, the last wick of light had been blown out of the poor woman's life.

I recalled what Devendra Mukherjee had told me. I turned to Janardan Maity and said, "Remember, Devendra Mukherjee had told us that he thought that the motive could be revenge? Do you think he knows about the accident?"

Janardan Maity calmed himself and sat down. "I don't know if he knows. But he himself is also on the list of liars," he said.

I was shocked once again. "Devendra Mukherjee?"

"Yes," Janardan Maity shut his eyes calmly. "He has lied to you."

"To me?" I was truly baffled. I tried to go over my conversations with him, but I didn't see what Janardan Maity was hinting at.

Janardan Maity looked at me intently for some time and asked a strange question, "Prakash, have you told me everything?"

"Wh-what do you mean?" I swallowed nervously.

Janardan Maity was still looking at me in the same intent

manner. "I had asked you to narrate to me everything that you had seen or heard since you came into the house yesterday, and to not leave anything out at all, however insignificant it may seem to you. But, have you told me everything?"

I weighed the question quite nervously. Clearly, he suspected that I may have left something out. Well, I may have. Because I was not at my best when I was talking to him. It was quite natural for me to have left out a minor detail. Was it, in reality, something important? Did it have a bearing on the murders? What on earth was it?

"I think I told you everything," I said nervously.

After staring at me for some more time, Janardan Maity shifted his gaze and said, "Well, I can obviously understand that it did not occur to you as something important. And I must say that I was quite lucky to have overheard it. Otherwise, we would have missed it altogether."

"What was it?" I asked, exasperated.

"Do you remember, when we were having dinner last night, you were seated between me and Devendra Mukherjee?"

"Yes."

"It was then that I overheard a bit of conversation between you and him."

"Which bit?" I asked curiously.

"You had asked him if Anita Mukherjee lived in an apartment in the city."

"Yes, that's right. And he said she did."

"And then, he said something else, didn't he?"

"Yes, I remember now. He said it was near Minto Park."

"No. You're still missing the point."

"What do you mean?"

"You're not saying what *he* had said."

"Well, what did he say?"

"He had said it was *somewhere* near Minto Park, although *he didn't know exactly where it was.*"

"Yes," I said, "you are right. That's what he said. But how does that make him a liar?"

Janardan Maity smiled and said, "He said he didn't know exactly where she lived. And yet, merely a few hours earlier, he had picked her up from her home!"

As the realization dawned on me, I gasped. "My God! Why, I never thought about that!"

Janardan Maity shrugged.

"But," I was bewildered, "why did he tell a lie?"

"I don't know."

"We can ask him, can't we?"

"Perhaps we can, but first, we must speak to someone else."

"Who?"

Janardan Maity rose from his chair and said, "Arun Mitra."

"Serves You Right"

We found Arun Mitra in his room. He welcomed us in and offered us chairs, while he himself sat on the bed. I looked around and remembered that I had come into this room last evening, before things had started falling apart. Arun and I had spoken at length. He had seemed so happy and cheerful then. As I looked at him now, it seemed to me that he was someone who had been ill for ages. His eyes had almost caved into his face. He seemed bewildered. His hair was all messed up too and he appeared a good ten years older than he actually was. He looked at me and Janardan Maity with a blank expression on his face. "What's the matter?" he asked.

"Well, you see, the matter," said Janardan Maity, "is that we have discovered your secret."

Arun shuddered. He placed his hands on his knees in order to steady them.

"What . . . what do you mean?"

"You know what I mean," Janardan Maity said in what I had come to think was his trademark calm voice. His piercing gaze seemed to be going right through Arun.

"No, I don't. I have no idea what you're talking about. What secret?" he made a defiant protest.

Janardan Maity shut his eyes and nodded his head from left to right. "There's no use denying it anymore, my friend. Cat's out of the bag. And now, it depends on you where you want it to go."

Arun Mitra's face looked so miserable that I actually felt sorry for him. But Janardan Maity went on. "The police suspect you for Anita's murder. You know that very well, don't you? They believe you stabbed her."

"But, I didn't, I didn't," yelled Arun. "She was already dead when I found her."

"You're lying, you killed her. And then, you came back to the hall and said that you found her dead."

"No! No! That's not true."

"Did you touch her?"

"No!"

"You're lying."

"I swear to God, I'm not lying."

"You. Are. Lying." Janardan Maity's voice boomed across the room.

"I did not touch her, trust me. I saw her, and all that . . . all that blood . . . and I . . ."

"You panicked?"

"Y-yes. I . . ."

"You panicked, and in your panic, you grabbed her arm and shook her violently, didn't you?"

"No. No, that's a lie."

"It's not a lie. The police found a bruise mark on her right arm, like someone had grabbed her by her wrist."

"I didn't touch her; it wasn't me."

"If it wasn't you, then who was it?"

"It was me!"

A voice behind us startled us. It was a calm voice and it was clear that the person who uttered those words was in complete control of herself. We turned around to see Preeti standing at the doorway. As she stepped into the room, it seemed to me that she had gone through an amazing transformation. Till now, I had noticed her only for her exotic beauty. But now, she seemed to me like the epitome of strength and reserve. She walked across the length of the room and came and stood by Arun Mitra. She put her hand softly on his shoulder and said once again, "It was me."

"No, Preeti," Arun looked at her pleadingly. "Please don't."

"Sshhh," she said, running her long nimble fingers through his hair. "Everything's going to be fine."

Arun Mitra shut his eyes and hung his head.

Preeti turned towards Janardan Maity and said in a grave manner, "It's easy to bully a man who is soft-spoken and mild-mannered. There's no bravado required in doing that, Mr. Maity."

Janardan Maity looked at her closely and smiled. He did not respond.

"It was I who grabbed her arm to check if she was alive. In my panic, I may have grabbed her too tight and may have left a mark on her arm."

Janardan Maity said, "Did you kill her?"

For a moment I saw Preeti's eyelids tremble, and she

blinked. Arun Mitra buried his head in his hands and clutched his hair.

Preeti's response came after a few seconds of hesitation, but when it did, her voice was so clear and determined that even Arun Mitra looked up at her in surprise.

"No, I did not!"

Janardan Maity looked at Arun keenly and said, "*He* doesn't seem to think so!"

Preeti's jaws hardened. "It does not matter what he thinks. I did not kill her."

Janardan Maity watched her closely for a few more seconds and said, "Well, we only have your word for it."

"What do you mean?"

"What I mean, Ms. Preeti," said Janardan Maity as he stood up and started walking up and down the room, "is that you had lied to us when you said that you were in the hall with Arun when the murder took place. The truth is that you were not there in the hall."

Preeti did not respond. Arun Mitra looked up at Janardan Maity. "She didn't lie, he said. "It was I who said th—"

"I must say I'm touched," Janardan Maity interrupted Arun midway, "by this sweet expression of selfless love. What do you think, Prakash?"

I swallowed hard. I had no idea what to say. But to avoid looking awkward, I said, "Oh yeah," and realized that it made me look more awkward than if I would have just remained silent. Janardan Maity went on. "The boy protects the girl, the girl shields the boy! Love in its purest and sweetest form. But that does not take anything away from the fact that both of you are liars."

The last few words were so emphatically said that for a

moment I thought the two lovebirds would crumble under pressure. But Preeti took Arun's hand in her own and clutched it strongly.

I looked at Janardan Maity and he looked at me. For a second, he seemed to be unsure of what to do or say next. Finally, he said, "So, you aren't going to tell me the truth, are you?"

"We can only tell you that we are innocent." Preeti's voice was firm.

Janardan Maity paused for a few moments and then said, "Very well, if you want to keep your mouth shut and shoot yourself in the foot, then so be it."

Having spoken these few words quite conclusively, he gestured towards me and turned around to leave. He had barely opened the door and taken a step outside when Preeti called out, "Mr. Maity?"

He stopped at the doorway and turned around.

"You're a good person, Mr. Maity," said Preeti, "and I know that you are an exceptionally intelligent man. You'll perhaps discover the truth one day. But I assure you that you will wish you hadn't."

Janardan Maity stared at her. I am sure her words meant something to him. Her lips were pursed and her face looked stern, yet devastatingly beautiful. I looked at her deep dark eyes and suddenly felt what an exceedingly lucky man Arun Mitra was. The strength of Preeti's character, her beauty, both intrinsic as well as that of her outer self, the way she carried herself . . . no, there was no way she could be the—

"Are you coming, Prakash?" Janardan Maity's call tore through my trail of thoughts and I excused myself from the young couple and joined him outside.

"What do you think?" I asked Janardan Maity, as we took the stairs to the ground floor.

"Tough nut to crack, that one," he said, under his breath.

"A very admirable woman, don't you think?" I said with a smile. "Somehow, she does not come across to me as being capable of committing such a nasty crime as murder."

Janardan Maity glanced in my direction. "Going by the rate at which you are striking people off your suspects list, I'm afraid you'll end up surrendering yourself to the Inspector by the time he comes in."

I took his remark in my stride and blushed. Really, no one in the house seemed to me to be capable of committing a murder, let alone two. I figured one needed to bear an infinite amount of malice to be able to commit a crime like that. If—I wondered—I was so shaken up by simply discovering a dead body, I could only imagine the tremendous amount of vice or anger needed within someone to be able to stab two people right through the chest. The sheer brutality that would be required to kill another human being! I tried to imagine the killer raising a dagger and stabbing Mr. and Mrs. Mukherjee in their hearts. I shuddered and shut my eyes.

We had reached the main hall when we saw Animesh Sen entering through the main door.

"This house arrest is intolerable," he said, "and disgusting, to say the least. I'm having to borrow cigarettes from the constables, can you believe that?"

Janardan Maity grinned. "Who says they only *take* bribes?"

Animesh Sen didn't seem to catch on to the sarcasm. Instead, he glanced around him to ensure that no one was around, and asked Janardan Maity in a whisper, "So, are the police arresting Preeti?"

Janardan Maity gave a measured response. "I am not sure, do you think they should?"

Animesh Sen let out a sigh. "Well, it's one thing to know in your gut that she did it. But all said and done, we don't have any evidence, now, do we?"

"Well, the police may have some," Janardan Maity said in a composed manner.

"Nah!" Animesh Sen chuckled nervously. "They won't find any."

Janardan Maity seemed to be feeling quite amused at this conversation, as was I. Despite what he had told us earlier, it was quite evident that he didn't really want any harm to come to Preeti. I also felt a little sorry for him. He was not a very intelligent man, and wore his emotions on his sleeve.

"Unless of course she has been so stupid as to tell them about the quarrel," Animesh Sen added.

"What?" Janardan Maity asked sharply. His expression changed. He held Animesh Sen by his arm and asked again, "What quarrel?"

Animesh Sen was quite taken aback at this sudden change in Janardan Maity's manner. He mumbled, "Nothing, I mean, nothing important."

"Mr. Sen," said Janardan Maity. "If you really want to save Preeti from the gallows, please, for heaven's sake, tell me everything you know. She is in grave danger."

Animesh Sen looked at Janardan Maity with a frown and freed his hand from Janardan Maity's clutch. "Grave danger? What the hell are you talking about?"

"I'm not saying anything. It is she who is admitting to have discovered Anita's body before Arun Mitra did," cried Janardan Maity.

A look of despair crept into Animesh Sen's face. He slapped his forehead and said, "Oh, that foolish, foolish girl," his face turning crimson in rage. "That miserable little stupid woman. And look who is she trying to protect? That blasted fellow, that non-entity, who's not even worth a penny!"

Janardan Maity pressed on. "Tell me, please, Mr. Sen. Tell me the truth."

Animesh Sen seemed to be in some sort of a dilemma. He hesitated for a few moments, and then asked Janardan Maity, "Mr. Maity, promise me she won't be harmed if I tell you the truth."

Janardan Maity put a soft assuring hand on Animesh Sen's shoulder. "I can promise you this—she will not be punished for a crime she has not committed."

Animesh Sen seemed relieved. His shoulders relaxed and he sat down on a couch. Janardan Maity and I sat next to him.

"I saw Preeti follow Mrs. Mukherjee into the dining room. Arun saw her too," Animesh Sen said with a sigh.

"Go on," prompted Janardan Maity.

"Of all the people who were in the party at that time, I was standing closest to the dining room. From the spot where I was standing, I couldn't see them, but I could hear them. They were quarrelling."

"Quarrelling?"

"Well, I don't know what you'd call it. You know these women, right? How, sometimes, they say stuff to each other in perfectly calm voices? We men, on the other hand, we are pretty straightforward. We will either sit down and have a beer together or cut each other's throat . . . er . . . pardon the expression. You know what I mean, right?"

"Yes," said Janardan Maity patiently.

"Yes, so, I mean men don't have mixed feelings, you know? No half emotions. It's either this way or that way. But women, oh they could be spewing venom at each other and smiling while at it."

"You were saying something about . . ."

"Yes, yes, I was coming to that. So, Preeti and Mrs. Mukherjee were saying stuff to each other. Although I couldn't hear them very well, I heard some of their . . . you know, conversation."

"You did?"

"Yes," said Animesh Sen.

"Would you mind telling me the exact words you heard?"

"Well, Mrs. Mukherjee was telling Preeti something like 'Don't think I don't know what you're up to', and then Preeti said something, which I couldn't quite catch, and then after sometime, Preeti said, 'No, you've got it all wrong.' And then, Mrs. Mukherjee said, 'I'm not blind, I can see what's happening. And I can't take this anymore, I'm going to have to talk to him about it'. Then, for quite some time, I couldn't hear anything. And then—"

"And then?" Janardan Maity asked. I noticed that there was a very pronounced frown on his forehead.

"Then, Preeti walked out of the dining room and joined us. But as she was walking out, she turned back and said something."

"What did she say?"

Animesh Sen looked straight at Janardan Maity and said, "She looked over her shoulder in sheer rage and said, 'Serves you right.'"

The Light

"Do you think he is telling the truth?" I asked Janardan Maity once Animesh Sen left. Janardan Maity had thanked him profusely after our conversation.

"I am not sure yet," he confessed. "You see, everything has a place of its own—all the bits and pieces, all the information, all the facts, the comments, the remarks, the evidence, the things you and I have seen and heard. But as long as we don't have *all* the pieces together, it is difficult, in fact impossible to reconstruct what really happened."

"You think there are still some pieces of the puzzle missing?" I asked.

Janardan Maity nodded. He seemed to be thinking deeply. The frown on his forehead was still there.

"There's something missing. Something . . ." he mumbled. "Or perhaps . . . perhaps there's something *I'm* missing. Something that I'm unable to see. Something hiding in the half-shadow."

As he said these words, his expressions changed. So far, he had been attentive beyond all measures. His eyes had been sharp, his movements had been swift, and it'd seemed impossible that even the most trivial detail—be it a harmless little word, an insignificant action, or a commonplace gesture—could escape his attention. But now, as he sat there thinking, he gave me the distinct impression that he was drowning, slowly yet surely, in a deluge of analytical reasoning. I could see that his mind was working things out, creating hypotheses, negating possibilities, and trying to inch towards the truth. And as he did so, his lips parted, the crease on his forehead became deeper and deeper, and his eyelids began to droop. He shook his head at times, nodded at others, and seemed to be generally lost in a completely different time and space. And then all of a sudden, he came out of his trance. He sat upright on his seat, took a deep breath, looked out of the nearby window, and gazed into the distance, all without saying a single word.

"What do you think we should do now?" I asked, finally.

After sometime, he said, "I think the rain has stopped. Perhaps a bit of fresh air will do us some good, what do you think?"

I nodded and said, "Yes, I, for one, am feeling suffocated in this house."

Janardan Maity didn't respond and walked away absent-mindedly, but towards the corridor instead of the main door. I realized he wanted to go towards the backyard. Since that was the only part of the house I had not seen yet, I decided to follow him. We had to go through the corridor where Anita Mukherjee's body had been discovered. In going past the spot where she had lain dead, I noticed an 'X' that the police had marked on the floor with chalk. The blood had been wiped off, but a faint outline of the stain still remained on the lime-green floor. A cold shiver went down my spine. I was keen to quicken my pace and walk past the spot, but I noticed that Janardan Maity stood at the unfortunate spot, and kept looking at the 'X' intently, lost in his thoughts. I walked right past him.

The rear side of the house did not seem to have any bedrooms. There was a door, and it was unlocked. I opened it to find myself peeping into a storeroom of sorts, stacked with housekeeping stuff and sacks of rice, pulses, and other food items. I shut the door and walked towards the next door to the south. This was the door that led to the backyard. The rain had stopped. I stepped out into a veranda. I looked left and right and figured that the same veranda ran all around the house. Mahadev's cottage was a few yards away, further towards the south, next to the garage.

"Aren't you going to join me?" I asked Janardan Maity as he finally came out and onto the veranda. "I intend to stretch my limbs and walk around a little bit."

He still seemed lost in his thoughts. Looking at me, he said, "No, you go ahead. I think I'll sit here for some time."

There was an armchair on the veranda. I saw him walk up to it and sit down. I looked at him and realized that he would now be processing all the bits and pieces of information that he had at his disposal and try to find the missing pieces. Those missing pieces, as he called them, seemed to bother him a lot, as was evident from the occasional grimace on his face and the frequent shaking of his head. I figured it was best that he be left alone.

I filled my lungs with fresh air. What a nasty business I had gotten myself into! And to think that I could have spent a perfect weekend reading that novel I had borrowed from the library and devouring the awesome cutlet that my servant makes. And instead, what was I doing? Walking around aimlessly in a house whose owners had been brutally murdered, not to forget that the police suspected me in one of the murders.

I walked around for a few minutes. The grass was wet and because of the rain, looked greener than it should have at this time of the year. I walked up to a Gulmohar tree and tugged at one of the low branches to give it a good shake. Hundreds of droplets of water immediately fell on my head and my body. Even with all the dreaded series of events, my mind suddenly felt quite light and free. It seemed to me that things would be all right, that the police would do their job well, that the real killer would be discovered and caught, and that I'd reach home safe and sound. Why I felt so, I could not tell. But I do remember feeling warm and comfortable, even if for a few seconds. But then, as I remembered the dagger rising out of my uncle's chest, my worries came rushing back to me.

Lost in my thoughts I continued ahead, when I spotted a puppy, a brown mongrel, wagging its tail. It had walked out of Mahadev's quarters. Must be his pet, I thought. The cottage was built of mud and had a thatch roof. I figured Mahadev must have had a rough night, in more ways than one. First the storm, and then the ghastly murders. The dog saw me looking at it and let out a short and sweet yelp. The old man stepped out of the cottage, saw me at a distance and came running across the yard to ask me if I needed anything.

"Oh no," I said. "Just wanted to check if your cottage was okay after last night's storm."

"Thank you for your concern, Babu. I did think at times

that the roof would blow away. But I recited the *Chaalisa* and God saved me."

I looked at him. He seemed like a devoted servant.

"How many years have you been here?" I asked him.

"It'll be fourteen years come *Phagun* this year, Babu."

"Where are you from?"

"Bihar, Babu. Purnia."

"You have served Chaudhuri madam and her husband too, haven't you?"

The expression on Mahadev's face changed. He hung his head and fidgeted with his hands. After sometime, he said softly, "Yes, Babu."

I hesitated for a few moments before asking, "There was an incident in this house . . ."

Mahadev joined his hands and looked at me with a pleading expression on his face. "Pardon my insolence, Babu, but please don't ask me anything more. I am not supposed to talk about anything. I am just a servant."

I looked at him for some time. "That's all right, I understand."

"Anything else, Babu?" he asked me. He seemed in a hurry to leave now.

"No, that's all. You may go."

Taking my gaze away from his retreating figure, I turned towards the veranda, to see Janardan Maity still lost in his thoughts. It was getting dark, I glanced at my watch to find that it was already five o'clock. I decided to walk around for some more time. The skies were still overcast, although things didn't look as threatening as they had last evening. It seemed the wind was blowing the dark clouds away. As I was looking around, I spotted someone standing at a window on the first floor. It was Preeti. She was making gestures with her hands and explaining something to someone, although the other person was not visible. The glass pane of the window was shut, so I couldn't hear anything that was being said. But there was something in her manner that told me that she was very excited. I analyzed the situation quickly. My biological compass told me that this couldn't be Arun Mitra's room, because that was on the other side—the Eastern side of the house. It couldn't be Nandita Chaudhuri's or Narendra's room either, because both were located on the ground floor. It could either be Devendra Mukherjee's or Animesh Sen's room.

I walked up to Janardan Maity and said excitedly, "Mr. Maity, come and take a look at this, quick."

"What is it?" He seemed quite irritated, as was evident from the grimace on his face and the rude manner of his speaking. It was quite evident I had disturbed his trail of thoughts.

Anyway, I explained to him what I had seen. Much to my surprise, he dismissed the entire thing with an irreverent scoff, and simply said, "I'm hunting for the solution, and you're hunting for more mysteries? That's Preeti's room."

I was quite ashamed at first. Really, why hadn't this occurred to me? "But of course, how silly of me," I said immediately with a shy grin. "I considered all the possibilities, except the one that was the most obvious."

Janardan Maity frowned and stared at me without saying a single word.

"I'm sorry if I disturbed you," I added.

But he still did not reply. He kept staring at me intently, and then simply ignored me—leaning back in his armchair and looking the other way. I felt a slight pang of anger. First things first, he had no business yelling rudely at me. How long had he known me, really? Secondly, I didn't like the way he had ignored me. It seemed quite a discourteous thing to do.

"I am going inside," I said coldly.

Janardan Maity looked at me and smiled, "I'm sorry, I must have been rude to you. Please forgive me. Actually, my thoughts have been extremely fickle today, and I'm quite upset at not being able to see the entire thing clearly. But I only have myself to blame for that. I do want to get to the bottom of all this, you know. And I really could use your help."

"What do you want me to do?" I was still quite upset.

"Nothing," he smiled with a spark in his eyes. "Just the pleasure of your company stimulates my brain. I have noticed this since last evening, and I see it again now. Please come and sit with me. Please."

His earnest requests placated me and I pulled up a chair and sat down beside him.

"Good," Janardan Maity said, "now let us go over the facts one by one, shall we?"

"Where do you want to start?"

"Wherever you want."

I thought it would be good to share with him the notes I had made earlier. "In the light of all the facts that have come to our knowledge," I began, "it seems that everyone in the house had a motive to murder Mr. and Mrs. Mukherjee."

"How did you arrive at that conclusion?" Janardan Maity asked patiently.

"Well, if Mr. Rajendra Mukherjee has made a will and if he has made provisions in that will, for say someone like—"

"That's," he interrupted, "one too many assumptions, don't you think?"

"Well then," I said, "if you don't want to talk about motive, then . . ."

"No, don't get me wrong, I do want to talk about motive. But not *only* about motive, you see, because, that lends a bias to the analysis of the facts at hand. More often than not, that route is steeped in assumptions. I'm sure, you'll agree with that."

"Yes, that's correct," I said.

"May I suggest another humble route?"

"Yeah, sure, please go ahead."

"Thank you. Let us consider the *facts* that lie in front of us. For instance, when Preeti was about to confess having grabbed Anita's body and turning her around, Arun Mitra said something like, 'No, please don't'. Didn't that strike you as a curious thing to say? What did he mean by that?"

I thought about it for some time. "Perhaps he pleaded with her not to take the blame for him?"

"Excellent explanation," said Janardan Maity, "or perhaps—and this is more likely—he thought that she had actually murdered Anita."

"My God! Really?" I exclaimed.

"Yes, do you see that this theory also explains why he was quick to provide an alibi for her last evening—a false one?"

"Yes . . . yes . . . I do see now."

Janardan Maity smiled.

"But there's one thing that I don't understand," I said.

"Which is?"

"Let's say Preeti murdered Mrs. Mukherjee. Why would she throw the dagger under Narendra's bed?"

"Once again, excellent question. I must say I'm very impressed. Tell me what would *you* have done?"

"I would have looked for a place where I could hide the dagger. But sure as hell I wouldn't have thought of Narendra's room as an ideal place to do so! What if he would have been awake?"

"Very good. Instead?"

"Well, I would have walked down the corridor, and hidden it in the store."

"Good, excellent analysis. But may I ask you something?"

"Sure."

"Why hide it at all?"

I was stumped. I juggled the question in my mind for some time. "Perhaps to cover my traces?" I said eventually.

Janardan Maity shook his head from left to right. "Do consider the fact that even if you were to hide it in the store, or in Preeti's case, under Narendra's bed, the police would be sure to find it, sooner or later."

"Well, that's true. What other reason could she have had to . . . to . . ."

Janardan Maity kept looking at me with a patient smile.

"Unless, of course, she *wanted* the dagger to be discovered."

"Right on target!" exclaimed Janardan Maity with a smile.

"You think that's what happened?"

"It is possible. In fact, in all likelihood, the finding of the bloodstained dagger under Narendra's bed seems to prove only one thing, and one thing alone—someone wanted to incriminate him in his stepmother's murder."

"But why would Preeti do it?"

"Ah, so now we come to the subject of the motive. You see, *now* we can discuss about it. Motive should always be discussed as a derivative of the facts at hand. One should never start a discussion with motive."

I remembered my notes and felt like a schoolboy who had put in a lot of effort into an elaborate homework only to find that his teacher had mercilessly put glaring red crossmarks all over his copybook the next day. I sighed, but Janardan Maity didn't seem to notice it.

"Indeed," he went on, "What motive could Preeti have in murdering Anita and implicating Narendra?"

"Money?" I suggested meekly.

"You are assuming Anita Mukherjee was rich. But I don't think she was. I think she depended on Raja for her day-to-day spends."

"Revenge?"

"For what?"

I fumbled. "I . . . uhh, I don't know."

"No, you're saying that because that's what Devendra Mukherjee felt. And because you liked the idea of revenge being the motive. This belief was further strengthened within your subconscious when we heard the tragic story of Nandita Chaudhuri. But do remember, my friend, that these are two totally different people. While revenge may have been a motive for Nandita Chaudhuri to kill Rajendra Mukherjee, we don't have anything to suggest that Preeti may have wanted to kill Anita Mukherjee to avenge something or someone."

"What other motive could she have had?" I thought out aloud. "Unless . . ."

"Yes?"

I recalled what Animesh Sen had told us about the scrap of conversation that he had overheard at the party. And the more I thought about it, the more I got excited. Yes! It made sense to me now. I felt the blood rush to my brains. It was all clear to me!

"What if," I turned to Janardan Maity and said, choosing my words carefully, "Preeti had felt threatened by Mrs. Mukherjee?"

"Care to explain?"

"Animesh Sen told us that he overheard a conversation between Preeti and Mrs. Mukherjee. From this conversation, we learn that Mrs. Mukherjee had confronted Preeti about the fact that she was flirting with my uncle. Mrs. Mukherjee asked her to stop what she was doing and threatened to confront my uncle as well."

"Go on," Janardan Maity said briefly. He seemed to be thinking hard. I was happy to see that for once my theory had caught his attention, and that he wasn't dismissing it altogether. I went on excitedly.

"When Preeti heard this, she panicked, she felt threatened. In her desperation, she picked up a dagger lying nearby and stabbed Mrs. Mukherjee."

Janardan Maity stared into the void for almost a minute. Then he said, "Perhaps!"

I was not very happy to receive such a timid and unenthusiastic response to such a brilliant reconstruction of what had happened last night. To me this seemed like the most logical explanation. The motive had not been money, nor had it been revenge. It had been *fear*!

But Janardan Maity didn't comment on the matter any further. Instead, he made an entirely disconnected remark. "You know something, Prakash?" he pinched his forehead and said, "The truth is always simple. Uncomplicated. What has happened has happened and it will stay that way. It will not change. And under normal circumstances, it would be very easy to get to the truth. The trouble begins when people start playing around with the truth. Because you don't know who to trust and who not to."

For the first time since last evening, Janardan Maity seemed quite frustrated. He was shaking his head again and again. His face looked quite haggard and tired.

I said, "Yes, I guess it's always a matter of trust, isn't it?"

"Who do *you* trust the most in this house, Prakash?"

"What do you mean? Like who would I confide in?" I asked.

"Not exactly. Who is the one person in the house, whose words you will believe?"

"Well, I couldn't say . . . That would depend."

"On what?"

"Well, it would depend on *what* is being said, I guess."

Janardan Maity looked at me curiously and shifted in his chair. "What do you mean?"

I said, "For instance, if Preeti were to tell me something about the history of Indian Art, I would probably believe her. Similarly, Nandita Chaudhuri knows a lot about roses. When it comes to roses and how they are grown, I would always believe what she says."

As I was saying these words, Janardan Maity was listening to me with rapt attention and with a very curious expression on his face. After some time, he looked away without making a comment. I realized he had perhaps intended to know something totally different when he asked me that question. Perhaps he wanted to know if I had believed Nandita Chaudhuri's story, or if I had thought what Animesh Sen had said about the overheard conversation was true. But when Janardan Maity spoke, his response seemed extremely surprising and enigmatic to me.

"Didn't I tell you that your presence stimulates my brain?" he said with a smile, as he took my hand in his hands and shook it earnestly, "Thank you, my friend, thank you. I was in the dark, but now, you have shown me the light."

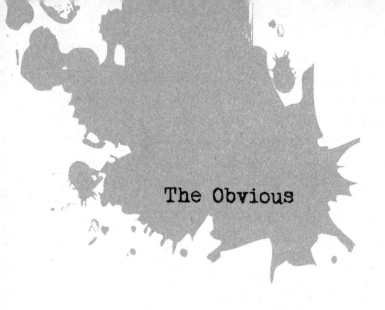

The Obvious

I was still trying to comprehend Janardan Maity's strange words, but I couldn't make head or tail out of them. I was about to ask him what he meant, when suddenly a constable stepped onto the veranda and announced that Inspector Sanyal had arrived and that everyone had been asked to assemble in the main hall.

Janardan Maity and I rose from our chairs. We walked behind the constable and reached the main hall to find that everyone had already gathered there. Arun and Animesh Sen were sitting together; Narendra was sitting with Devendra Mukherjee, while Preeti sat with Nandita Chaudhuri.

Inspector Sanyal showed us a couch; Janardan Maity and I took our seats.

I looked around the hall and noticed a certain amount of tension in everyone's manner. I myself was quite tensed, because as far as Rajendra Mukherjee's murder was concerned, my own fate was now hanging by a thin line. Everyone else, without exception, had a watertight alibi. It had been a long and nerve-wracking twenty-four hours for me in this bungalow. But now that Inspector Sanyal was here, we could expect to get some news of a breakthrough in the case. I hoped and prayed that he would have the good sense to believe my story.

Inspector Sanyal spoke to his constables in whispers for some time. Then, he stood in the middle of the hall, and said, "From our initial reports, we have established the cause of death. Both the deaths have been due to stabbing with a sharp instrument. The timings of both deaths have been established too. In the case of Mrs. Anita Mukherjee, it has been estimated between eleven o'clock in the night and one o'clock, and in case of Mr. Rajendra Mukherjee, we could narrow it down to between midnight and two o'clock. Now, you are all educated and smart individuals, and as you may be aware by now, all of you are suspects in the murders of Rajendra Mukherjee and his wife, Anita Mukherjee. The facts of the case are as follows.

"At around half past ten last night, more than one of you had seen Mrs. Anita Mukherjee take dinner to her stepson, Mr. Narendra's, room. Around forty or forty-five minutes later, Mr. Arun Mitra found Mrs. Mukherjee lying dead in a pool of blood in the corridor outside Mr. Narendra's room, towards the rear portion of the house. The victim had been stabbed to death, but the murder weapon was nowhere to be seen. Minutes later, three of you, namely Prakash Ray, Devendra Mukherjee, and Janardan Maity found the murder weapon underneath the bed of Mr. Narendra Mukherjee, who later claimed ignorance about how it had ended up there. We searched Mr. Narendra's room and found an empty bottle of whisky, a wristwatch, a packet of cigarettes and a matchbox—both soaked in water—

and finally a wallet with very little money in it. We also found several stubs of betting tickets in his pockets. These go to prove that not only had Mr. Narendra been drinking last night, but that he had also been betting heavily on horses recently. Quite a few of you have also said that when he had come into the house last night, he was drunk."

Inspector Sanyal paused to catch his breath. I passed a sweeping look around the room. Everyone was listening with rapt attention. My eyes finally returned to the inspector, and I was startled to find that he was looking straight at me. He said, "The second murder was discovered by Mr. Prakash Ray. Prior to this, it is important to note that Mr. Narendra had assaulted Animesh Sen, who had accused him of having murdered the first victim. The commotion was contained, and Mr. Ray went up to check on Rajendra Mukherjee. It has been claimed unanimously that he took an unusually extended amount of time to check on Mr. Mukherjee, although Mr. Ray himself claims that he had stopped by his own room upstairs to drink a couple of glasses of water. And when he did return to the hall, he claimed to have found Mr. Mukherjee dead. As in the previous murder, the victim had been stabbed through the heart, the only difference being, this time, the murder weapon was found on the victim's body."

Inspector Sanyal now took two pouches from one of the constables' hands and held them up.

"We found two murder weapons. This dagger was used to commit the first murder. It was found underneath Narendra Mukherjee's bed minutes after the murder was discovered. The other dagger was used to murder Rajendra Mukherjee. It was found on the victim's body."

He handed over the pouches to the constable and

continued. "So far, we have found only one piece of evidence, other than the murder weapons. It was actually found on Mrs. Mukherjee's person. There's a bruise on her right arm, clearly made by the hands of her assailant—who took her by surprise by grabbing her arm from behind and then stabbing her in the chest. Now, based on preliminarily facts and evidence, the principal suspect in the murder of Mrs. Anita Mukherjee is her stepson, Narendra Mukherjee. It is possible that the victim had entered his room with the dinner tray. An argument may have brewed up and Mr. Narendra could have assaulted the victim with a dagger in a fit of drunken rage. He may or may not have intended to kill her, and the entire thing may have been an accident. But nevertheless, the fact is that she did die. In the struggle, Narendra could have grabbed her, which left a bruise on her arm. On finding her dead, he may have panicked and in a bid to hide the murder weapon hastily, he threw it under his bed, hoping to dispose it off when he would get the chance.

"Similarly, the principal suspect in the murder of Mr. Rajendra Mukherjee is Mr. Prakash Ray. The victim was lying asleep in his bed. It has been unanimously claimed by everyone that Mr. Ray himself offered to go and check on his uncle. When he entered his uncle's bedroom, he had ample time to murder him with the dagger. We are also investigating into any possible links that Mr. Ray may have had in the past with Narendra Mukherjee. It is highly likely that these were pre-planned murders. But since we do not have conclusive evidence yet, we would like to continue interrogating these two suspects and carry on our investigation. Mr. Ray, Mr. Mukherjee, you'll need to come with us to the station. As for the rest of you . . . you are free to go for now, but I emphasize that you are not allowed to leave the city of Kolkata without informing me."

I was dumbstruck. Hadn't Janardan Maity said that the police were investigating under the assumption that there was only one murderer? Did this mean that I was about to be arrested?

"Inspector Sanyal," Janardan Maity interjected.

"Yes?"

"May I say something?" he asked politely.

"What do you want to say?" The Inspector asked curiously.

"If you don't mind, I'd like to shed some light on the murders."

There was a stunned silence in the room. Everyone looked at Janardan Maity, but no one spoke. I was certain that the Inspector would not allow him to speak, but I was surprised to see that he threw a sweeping glance around the room and nodded his head.

My heart was racing. I had never ever been to a police station before, let alone been arrested, that too for murder. I didn't have any friends in the city who could come and bail me out. I realized I was in deep trouble. Right now, my only hope was the man who was now standing in the middle of the hall, facing us.

Janardan Maity took a few moments to look around the room. He must have sensed the tension, but he didn't dwell on it. Instead, he cleared his throat and began.

"Thank you, Inspector Sanyal. Over the last twenty-four hours or so, quite a few facts have come to my knowledge. I am of the opinion that these facts have direct bearing upon this case, and I believe my presenting them in front of the police in an orderly fashion may help you in solving this baffling mystery. If anyone in this room has any objection to anything I am about to say, please feel free to interrupt me at any point."

There was pin-drop silence in the room. Janardan Maity went on: "When Prakash was having a conversation with Anita last night, she mentioned that Mrs. Chaudhuri had to sell this bungalow to Rajendra Mukherjee after an accident. I learnt about this conversation from Prakash, and to me that seemed like a very curious thing to say. What accident was she referring to? Hadn't Mrs. Chaudhuri sold the house after her husband's death? That's what all of us know, isn't it? Because that's what Rajendra Mukherjee had always told us. And we also know that Mrs. Chaudhuri's husband had died of cancer. To me it seemed quite odd that someone would refer to a death by cancer as an accident."

My eyes caught Nandita Chaudhuri. As usual, she was holding her head upright. But now, her face looked exceedingly stern.

"But, as you will learn this evening, there are a lot of dirty secrets in this house," Janardan Maity went on, "and what you are about to hear is just one of them. I later learnt that indeed, there *was* an accident in this house. A violent, nasty incident. Would you care to tell us about it, Mrs. Chaudhuri?"

All eyes turned towards Nandita Chaudhuri now. But she didn't speak.

"If you won't tell them," said Janardan Maity politely, "I'll be forced to."

"Mr. Maity," Nandita Chaudhuri's voice filled the hall as she spoke in clearly enunciated words. "I can't hold you back from doing anything. You may do as you please."

"Very well then," said Janardan Maity, taking charge of

the room once again, "I have learnt this morning, from none other than Mrs. Chaudhuri herself, that her daughter had died in this house at the foot of those stairs. She would have been seven today."

Everyone looked at Nandita Chaudhuri in shock, who, in turn, looked devastated. Her face had the most wrenching look of grief written on it. Inspector Sanyal was just about to say something, when we were all startled by a cry from the other side of the hall.

"Stop, please stop!"

All eyes turned to the person who had shouted out those words. It was Narendra Mukherjee. He had buried his face in his palms.

But Janardan Maity didn't stop. "Five years ago, when he was a tenant in this house, Rajendra Mukherjee had a quarrel with his son. They were both drunk. Rajendra Mukherjee hit his son and he fell on a grand piano, which tumbled down the stairs and crushed Mrs. Chaudhuri's daughter to death."

Gasps of horror were heard from various parts of the room, but Inspector Sanyal continued to listen impassively to Janardan Maity, who carried on with complete indifference. "Would it be too far-fetched for me to assume that you wanted to avenge your daughter, Mrs. Chaudhuri?"

"No. No. No. For heaven's sake, stop!" Narendra screamed out, his face still buried in his palms.

"Tell us, Mrs. Chaudhuri." Janardan Maity demanded a response.

"Yes, I wanted to kill Narendra!" Nandita Chaudhuri suddenly yelled out.

I had never seen her in such a form. She had stood up and was swaying back and forth. Her eyes were burning, the nerves on her throat had all swollen up, and her temples were throbbing visibly. She gnashed her teeth as she spoke.

"I wanted to kill him, so that his father could know what it is like to lose a child. I wanted to kill his only child so that the great Rajendra Mukherjee could know that all the money in this world could not possibly make one forget the beautiful face of one's child. Yes, I wanted to kill him!"

The entire room seemed to shake with the force with which Nandita Chaudhuri made her confession.

"But . . . but . . ." stammered Nandita Chaudhuri.

"But what, Mrs. Chaudhuri?" Janardan Maity asked softly.

"I . . . I couldn't . . ."

My stomach suddenly seemed empty, very empty. And my knees seemed weak.

"I couldn't bring myself up to do it," Nandita Chaudhuri muttered, as if her voice was coming from a faraway place, "I simply couldn't."

"I-I am so sorry . . . so sorry." Narendra sobbed like a child.

Janardan Maity took a step closer to Mrs. Chaudhuri and softly placed a hand on her shoulder.

"You couldn't because you are too good to commit a heinous crime like murder, madam," he said. "And you kept coming back to this house because you had your daughter's memories strewn everywhere around the place, isn't it?"

Tears started rolling down Nandita Chaudhuri's face. She broke down. Preeti made her sit next to herself and tried her best to console her. Narendra was in bad shape too. Devendra Mukherjee patted his back and tried to console him.

Janardan Maity turned towards the rest of us and said, "No, Mrs. Chaudhuri didn't murder anyone. But there's one more thing that has caught my attention over the last twenty-four hours. I'd like to ask a few questions to my learned friend Animesh Sen."

"What questions, Mr. Maity?" Animesh cleared his throat and asked.

"You told me that you had overheard a conversation between Ms. Preeti and Mrs. Anita Mukherjee just before Mrs. Mukherjee was found dead. Apparently, they were having some sort of a showdown. Am I correct?"

"Well, I am not quite . . ." Animesh Sen fumbled.

"Would you care to tell us what exactly you heard?"

"Listen, Mr. Maity," said Animesh Sen. "I don't think I . . ."

"Well, I can understand the reason for your hesitation. But I need to share what you heard with everyone present here, because it's important. And seeing that you are not inclined to tell us yourself, I will narrate to everyone what you told me. Prakash was witness to the discussion between you and me, but still, if you feel that I am saying something incorrect, please stop me right away."

Animesh Sen tried to make one last protest but it fell on deaf ears. Janardan Maity continued. "Last night, after Mrs. Mukherjee walked into the dining room, Preeti walked into the room too. There were at least three people who saw her do so—Animesh Sen, Arun Mitra, and myself. But since Mr. Sen was standing closest to the dining room, he overheard bits of the conversation that took place between the two women. This is what Mr. Sen heard: Preeti said something to Mrs. Mukherjee and Mrs. Mukherjee replied, 'Don't think I don't know what you're up to.' And then Preeti said something. There was a lot of noise all around, everyone in the main hall was talking and laughing, so Mr. Sen couldn't catch what she said. After sometime, he heard Preeti say, 'No, no, you've got it all wrong.' And then, Mrs. Mukherjee said, 'I'm not blind; I can see what's happening. And I can't take this anymore, I'm going to have to talk to him about it.' After this, for almost four-five minutes, Mr. Sen didn't hear anything. And then . . .''

Janardan Maity looked at Preeti, who looked back at him without any hesitation in her expressions.

"Then," continued Janardan Maity, "Preeti came out of the dining room, turned back and said, 'serves you right'."

"That's utter nonsense," cried out Arun Mitra. "How do you know this man is telling you the truth, Mr. Maity?"

Animesh Sen pinched his forehead and shook his head in frustration. I don't think he had ever imagined that Janardan Maity would divulge the conversation to the police. I looked at Preeti and saw that her expression had not changed one bit and that she was looking straight at Animesh Sen.

Inspector Sanyal turned towards Animesh Sen and asked in a composed voice, "Mr. Sen, you do understand the importance of your statement, don't you? Now tell me, is this true?"

Animesh Sen shut his eyes and fumbled as he spoke. "I heard those words but . . . I . . . didn't mean to."

Arun Mitra yelled out yet again. "This is ridiculous! The man is lying!"

"He is *not* lying!" Janardan Maity's voice rose several levels and echoed through the hall. "He has heard those words. I'll prove it to you soon."

There was pin-drop silence in the room once again. Inspector Sanyal now spoke in a calm yet no-nonsense manner. "Mr. Maity, I would like to know right now, exactly what this conversation has to do with this case?"

"Sure, Inspector! I shall explain. But before that please allow me the indulgence of telling you one more thing, if you permit?"

Inspector Sanyal let out a deep sigh and cautioned, "Okay, but this better be relevant."

"Thank you." Janardan Maity smiled. "You see right from the time I saw Narendra in his room last night with the dagger under his bed, one question has bothered me again and again—what made him kill his stepmother? Just rage? Or a drunken state? It seemed quite unlikely to me, especially given the way she was murdered. We all know Narendra hated his stepmother, but why would he want to kill her in the middle of a house full of people and then throw the dagger under his own bed? He was drunk, no doubt, but he was not *so* drunk. Moreover, I have questioned Mahadev about the two daggers and he has told me that he has never seen them before. In other words, in all likelihood, they were brought into the house from outside. Inspector, this is where I don't agree with your theory of the accidental assault."

"What do you mean?" Inspector Sanyal asked.

"Let us assume for a moment that there was an argument between Anita Mukherjee and Narendra Mukherjee, and in the heat of the moment, Narendra flashed a dagger that he had on his person and stabbed his stepmother with it. But why would he be carrying *two* identical daggers? There could be only one possible reason for that: he wanted to commit *two* murders, not one, and that both the murders were pre-planned. But if that were to be true, why would he throw the first dagger under his own bed after stabbing Mrs. Mukherjee? Wouldn't he want to hide it? No, Inspector, the entire hypothesis is an exercise in contradictions. It does not seem to me that Narendra murdered his stepmother on an impulse. Nor does it seem to me that he did so in a pre-planned manner. In fact, I don't think it was he who murdered Anita Mukherjee."

Preeti now spoke, her voice as composed as ever. "Mr. Maity, do you remember the events of last night?"

"Yes, I do, Preeti."

"Then please answer a question of mine: if Narendra didn't murder Mrs. Mukherjee and throw the dagger under his bed, then that would mean that someone else did so, right?"

"Absolutely right!"

"Fine, so who was it?" Preeti asked. "Everyone else present in the house was in this hall when she was murdered, including myself. Who killed Anita Mukherjee and threw the dagger under Narendra's bed?"

"No one!" said Janardan Maity.

The answer came so suddenly, and was so unexpected, that for a few seconds everyone was dumbstruck. I myself was quite taken aback. I knew he was a strange man, but what on earth was he trying to say?

"No one? What nonsense, Mr. Maity," Animesh Sen said in an insolent manner. "Are you saying it was an accident?"

"No, Mr. Sen, it wasn't an accident. It wasn't a murder, and it wasn't suicide either," said Janardan Maity, his small eyes burning in excitement.

There were soft dismissive murmurs around the room as people started to crosstalk. Inspector Sanyal seemed quite annoyed too, and took a couple of steps towards Janardan Maity and asked him to sit down. Animesh Sen scoffed and remarked, "Mr. Maity, I don't know if you know this, but I used to admire you very much, because it had seemed to me that you are an exceptionally intelligent man, but what you are saying right now isn't making any sense to anyone in this room at all."

Janardan Maity turned towards Animesh Sen. "Thank you for your appreciation, Mr. Sen," he began. "But it seems I do not deserve your kind words of praise. Because, you see, I am not intelligent at all. Had I been intelligent, would I not have been able to see the obvious truth that had been staring me at my face since last night? No, Mr. Sen, I am an ordinary man, and it is in the very nature of ordinary men not to see the obvious. Don't you see? The murderer of Rajendra Mukherjee was his wife Mrs. Anita Mukherjee."

What Really Happened

I think it was pretty much at that point when everyone in the room concluded that Janardan Maity had lost his mind. Even in this grave hour, there were soft dismissive chuckles heard from various corners of the room. The only person who didn't seem even the least bit amused was Inspector Sanyal, who wore a distinctive frown and stared intently at Janardan Maity with a fixed gaze.

Animesh Sen was so taken aback, that he couldn't even ask Janardan Maity what on earth he meant.

Arun Mitra said, "What are you saying, Mr. Maity? How can Anita Mukherjee murder Mr. Rajendra Mukherjee? Are you saying her ghost went up to his bedroom upstairs and stabbed him?"

Janardan Maity turned to Arun and said, "No, all I am saying is that when we found Anita Mukherjee in the corridor last evening, she was alive."

Once again, we were all so amazed that no one could speak. Even the Inspector seemed dumbstruck.

Finally, the reticent Devendra Mukherjee said in an irritated voice, "Listen Mr. Maity, this has gone on for too long now. Will you please sit down and let the police do their job?"

"I will sit down for sure, oh most definitely I will. But only when I have seen cuffs on the wrists of the person who planned my dear friend's murder, not before that." Janardan Maity's voice rang clear and distinctly across the room, so much so, that the low whispers were all silenced.

Devendra Mukherjee was still staring at Janardan Maity with the irritated look on his face. "Let's think logically about what you are suggesting. You are saying Anita was alive when Arun found her body?"

"Yes," said Janardan Maity calmly.

"Very well. Can you please explain to everyone present here, under what circumstances can four men, first Arun, then myself, then yourself, and finally Prakash, all of us who had seen her up close, mistake a living woman as a corpse?"

"Under two special circumstances, sir. Under two *very* special circumstances."

"Indeed? And what might they be?"

"First," Janardan Maity raised a finger, "if the woman has been an actress, especially on the stage. Why, haven't you read this?

What noise is this? Not dead? Not yet quite dead?
I that am cruel am yet merciful,
I would not have thee linger in thy pain.'"

Everyone present in the room watched Janardan Maity with absolute awe and wonder as he recited the lines.

"Othello – Act 5 Scene 2. Desdemona lying dead, smothered by her husband. Yes, Desdemona! A part that Anita used to play so well, and a part whose flawless portrayal had made Raja fall in love with her."

Devendra Mukherjee was listening calmly, with a sarcastic smile on his face. "Amusing, to say the least, this theory of yours. And what, pray, is the second circumstance, Mr. Maity?"

"Ah, the second circumstance. Devilish, cruel, yet terrifyingly simple. The announcement of death by a doctor!"

Very, very gradually, the smile of amusement disappeared from Devendra Mukherjee's face and he began to tremble in sheer rage. "What are you trying to say? You, you . . . s-scoundrel!"

Janardan Maity didn't seem bothered at all. On the contrary, he stepped forward and bent down towards Devendra Mukherjee's face and said in a clear, unhesitant voice, "I'm saying Dr. Mukherjee, that *you* orchestrated the murder of your brother Rajendra Mukherjee, and that *you* stabbed his wife Anita Mukherjee to death."

Devendra Mukherjee was so livid, that he was barely able to speak. I had never seen such a transformation in a man's personality. His face suddenly seemed so cruel and nastily contorted, that it seemed like the devil himself was sitting in a chair across the room.

Janardan Maity went on. "Anita, your brother's second wife, had fallen in love with you after she came to India, isn't it, Dr. Mukherjee? And during one of your secret rendezvous, she must have told you about the enormous wealth that your brother had amassed in his career. It was then that the idea of murdering your brother occurred to you. I must say I am amazed at the amount of planning you had done to get to your brother's fortune. The job would have been really easy for you, because Anita was in love with you and all that you needed to do was to murder Raja, which could have been achieved by a simple framed road accident. But there were two problems that you were facing. First, you never truly loved Anita, and had no intentions of marrying her. Moreover, it was she who would have inherited Raja's wealth, not you, and you didn't trust her to let you enjoy that wealth. Second, if Rajendra Mukherjee would have been killed and if you would have married his widow, then naturally the two of you would have come under suspicion. You wanted the money, but you wanted to enjoy it in peace, not under constant heat from the law. It was then, that unknown to Anita, you devised your fiendish plan. Your plan was to kill not just your brother, but his wife as well. You would convince Anita to kill her husband, and you would then kill her, and you would frame Raja's son for the murders, making it seem like the drunk and unruly son killed his father and stepmother to avenge the death of his mother. If you'd have been able to pull this off, the entire wealth that your brother possessed would come to you, and there wouldn't be a shred of doubt cast on you."

Janardan Maity stopped for a moment to catch his breath. Before anyone could say anything, he went on. "But again, this presented a problem, didn't it, Dr. Mukherjee? Even if things were to go as per your plan, there was still a risk of your lover being suspected for her husband's murder, and you being suspected for hers. You couldn't take that risk. You couldn't allow any kind of suspicion to befall you, however little and insignificant that may have been. Which is why, you needed something that would ensure that you aren't suspected at all—you needed *alibis!* You created the most perfect one for yourself and your lover. She *pretended* to be dead and you being a doctor, your confirmation of her death was accepted and believed by everyone, including me. You also ensured that no one touched the corpse or came too near to it. You even covered it with a curtain, didn't you? All of these created an impression that she was dead, when in reality, she was alive. As a result, there were eyewitnesses, vouching for the fact that when Anita Mukherjee died, you were amidst several other people in a party. That was your alibi for Anita's murder. When you gathered everyone else in the main hall and engaged them in a game of deductive logic about who the murderer of Anita could be, she played her part in the second act. She rose from her position, and went upstairs to kill her husband, with a dagger that she had hidden in the bedroom that very morning. Your plan was so cruel, that to make her job easier, you had even put your brother to sleep with a sedative, so that there would be no struggle at all."

All around the room, people gasped at the shocking description of the doctor's crime, but Janardan Maity continued.

"After accomplishing her job, Anita resumed her position. And then came the third and final act of your ruthless plan. I believe you had convinced Anita that you would bribe the men who would come with the police to take her 'corpse' away. You had told her that they would take you to safety and you would meet her later after the dust settled. Little did she know that this was a lie, and that you would excuse yourself with the pretext of making a call to the police and would use that time to go to Narendra's empty room, fetch the dagger from under the bed, stab Anita to death with it, and throw the dagger back under the bed. She lay there pretending to be dead, not knowing that death itself was swooping down on her in the most unexpected manner. You see, she had made the mistake of loving a man who didn't love her at all."

Inspector Sanyal had been silent so far. He now interrupted, "But why do you think he did all this, Mr. Maity?"

"As I said earlier, Inspector, to create the perfect alibi for himself and his lover" replied Janardan Maity. "His alibi was that at the *perceived* time of both deaths, he was nowhere near either of the victims. At the time of Anita's death, the perceived time, mind you, he was in this hall with everyone else. And at the time of Raja's murder too, he was here in this hall, amidst everyone else. No one bothered to check where he was at the time when Anita was actually murdered, because no one knew *when* she was actually murdered. Now let us consider Anita. Her alibi was that at the time of the murder that she really committed, she was dead! No alibi in the world could be more perfect than that, don't you think Inspector? Dr. Mukherjee needed an alibi for her, even though he was going to kill her anyway, just to ensure that no suspicion would ever be cast upon him. I must say it was a very, very clever plan."

"But where does Narendra figure in all this?" Inspector Sanyal asked.

"As per the plan, Anita was entrusted with planting the dagger under Narendra's bed before she took up her position in the corridor. And that's what she did. She checked if he was sleeping, then she poured blood all over herself and in the corridor and on the dagger, and then pushed the bloodstained dagger under his bed. This made it seem that Narendra had killed his stepmother in a fit of drunken rage. It is also my belief that in this entire plan, Anita's own blood was used. I don't know if anyone else has noticed, but there were puncture marks on both her arms. Dr. Mukherjee knew that the blood found at the crime scene would be tested by forensics, and he made sure that real blood was drawn beforehand from Anita's body and used in the entire charade."

"But tell me one thing, Mr. Maity. When and how did you suspect that the doctor had a hand in this?" asked the Inspector.

"There were plenty of things that aroused my suspicion, Inspector. The first was the dagger. To me, it felt like *too obvious* a clue to leave behind, even for a man who was stone drunk. I myself, and some people in this room, would vouch for the fact that Narendra was not so drunk that he would be foolish enough to commit a murder and then hide the murder weapon under his bed. Had he been so drunk, he would not have been able to commit the murder in the first place. The two things seemed quite contradictory to me, right from the beginning. It was this that made me wonder: should my question be who would benefit from Rajendra Mukherjee's death? Or should it be, who would benefit if his son went to the gallows?"

"I see, what else?" asked Inspector Sanyal.

"The second was the telephone. I had seen Mrs. Chaudhuri come out of the study last evening, and I have learnt from her that although she had pretended to make a call to her daughter, in reality she made a call to her friend in the city, with whom she lives. I have verified this personally. That call went through, as did Devendra Mukherjee's call to the police. Why, then, did my call not go through? Was it simply because of the storm, or was there foul play involved, in order to keep the police away for some more time for the second murder—the real murder of Anita Mukherjee—to be committed?

"The third was the conversation that Animesh Sen had overheard. Arun, didn't I tell you that he had really heard those words? You see, there's one fact that you perhaps do not know. Animesh Sen was in love with Preeti. But he soon found out that Preeti is in love with you. Needless to say, Mr. Sen was heartbroken. Unfortunately, there was someone who had discovered this even before I did. And that someone was Devendra Mukherjee. It was he who had suggested to Animesh Sen that the lady he was in love with was an incorrigible flirt, and that she and Rajendra Mukherjee were having an affair."

"But, Mr. Maity," Inspector Sen interjected, "why would he want to make such a suggestion to Animesh Sen? What did he gain by doing so?"

Janardan Maity turned towards Animesh and smiled. "For information, Inspector Sanyal, valuable information."

The Inspector seemed confused, especially because Animesh grimaced and clutched his own hair in despair.

"Information about what?" asked the Inspector.

Janardan Maity smiled, his piercing gaze still fixed on Animesh Sen. "Information about Rajendra Mukherjee's will. Am I correct, Mr. Sen? After he suggested that Preeti was having an affair with his brother, didn't Dr. Mukherjee ask you if he has made a will? A question, which when asked under any other circumstance would have sounded extremely suspicious to you, or to anyone else. But now, burning with rage, you gave him that information, flouting all norms of client-attorney confidentiality. You told him that Rajendra Mukherjee had not made a will yet. Isn't that so, Mr. Sen?"

Animesh Sen didn't respond, but it was quite evident that Janardan Maity's claims were correct. He went on. "Once he knew that there was no will, Devendra Mukherjee set in motion his devious plan. It is also my belief that Devendra Mukherjee must have used this suggestion about the affair between Preeti and his brother to incite Anita Mukherjee as well, just to ensure that she didn't feel any pangs of conscience in murdering her husband."

"But I don't understand . . . what about this conversation?" asked Inspector Sanyal curiously.

"Ah yes, the conversation that Animesh Sen overheard. That conversation is a bizarre and fascinating example of the force of suggestion and the tricks that it can play on your mind, especially when your mind is weak and bruised. You see Devendra Mukherjee's suggestion had made Animesh extremely frustrated and restless. The woman he had worshipped like a goddess, she was flirting around with not one but two men, one of them old enough to be her father. Imagine what must be going through his mind. And in that mental state, he overheard—heard, mind you, not saw— portions of a conversation between two women. And he heard what his mind *wanted to hear*."

"What do you mean?" asked the Inspector.

"It's perfectly simple. Animesh Sen hears Mrs. Mukherjee challenging Preeti: *'Don't think I don't know what you're up to.'* But in reality, it was Preeti who said that to Mrs. Mukherjee. I believe she had discovered that Anita was having an affair with Devendra. Then Animesh hears the words, *'No, no, you've got it all wrong,'* and he immediately assumes that it was Preeti who was trying to give an explanation to Anita, when in reality, it was just the other way round. It doesn't end there, because again after sometime, he hears someone say, '*I'm not blind, I can see what's happening. And I can't take this anymore, I'm going to have to talk to him about it.*' Animesh assumes that Anita is saying these words and that she was threatening to confront her husband about his alleged affair with Preeti. But, again, in reality, it is just the other way round. Preeti had nothing but genuine respect and admiration for Raja and looked up to him as a father figure. When she learnt about Anita's affair, she threatened to expose her to Raja, because she couldn't see him get hurt."

Animesh Sen hung his head. "I'm sorry, I really am. I didn't think—"

"You should, Mr. Sen," said Janardan Maity. "You should. It is a rare and admirable habit—thinking."

Janardan Maity turned towards the rest of us and went on. "The final clue was the most incriminating. You see I had known Raja closely for some time. He was a strong man. I believe when Anita Mukherjee entered his room in the dark and stabbed him, the pain woke him up from his sedative-induced sleep, and he grabbed the arm that had stabbed him; his wife's arm. Although it was only for a brief period of time, perhaps a few seconds, the strong grip of a dying man left a bruise on her right arm. She panicked in the dark and left the room. She quickly resumed her position, put the curtain on top of herself in a hurry and played the 'corpse'. But what she didn't realize was that the bruise was now beginning to appear on her arm, for such is the nature of bruises. When I had first seen Anita lying 'dead' in the corridor, the bruise was not there on her right arm. But when the police arrived and her body was being examined, it was there. The sudden appearance of the bruise had seemed odd to me, but I hadn't thought much of it because post-mortem bruising from ante-mortem causes are not uncommon. But I had made the mistake of assuming that the bruise must have been caused by the murderer. It was only later that I realized that it was caused by the victim!"

Goodbyes

In less than ten minutes after Janardan Maity had peeled the mask off Devendra Mukherjee's face, the doctor broke down and pleaded guilty to the charge of murdering Anita Mukherjee, and to that of aiding and abetting the murder of his brother, Rajendra Mukherjee. But all of us took quite some time to fully comprehend the devilish plan that the doctor had hatched, and the extraordinary intelligence with which Janardan Maity saw through it.

By the time Dr. Mukherjee was taken away by the police, it was already 8 o'clock, and Janardan Maity remarked that it was quite late and that everyone should stay back for the night. We all agreed.

At dinner, although everyone was present, no one spoke. I myself was going over and over the brutal misdeeds of the doctor and shuddered to realize that he had almost gotten away with it. But for Janardan Maity, Narendra and I would have been sitting in the lock-up by now.

After dinner, Janardan Maity and I stood in the main hall, having a conversation about next morning's transport arrangements, when Nandita Chaudhuri walked up to us.

"Mr. Maity," she said in a soft voice, "I want to thank you for everything."

"Oh no, Mrs. Chaudhuri," said Janardan Maity, "please don't thank me. I wish I could do more for you."

A sad, almost unnoticeable smile appeared on the woman's lips and she sighed. Janardan Maity looked keenly at her and then took a step towards her, and spoke in a very soft voice. "Mrs. Chaudhuri, if I ask you for something, will you give it to me?"

Nandita Chaudhuri looked at him with her deep, beautiful eyes and said, "Me? I have nothing to give you, Mr. Maity. Nothing."

"Oh, but you do, Mrs. Chaudhuri, you do."

"I have lost everything, Mr. Maity. What can I possibly give you?" Nandita Chaudhuri seemed perplexed.

Janardan Maity looked into her eyes and said, "You can give me your word, madam, that you will never ever return to this house again."

Nandita Chaudhuri stared at the strange man in front of her for a long time. Her eyes seemed to search Janardan Maity's soul for what his words really meant. And I think she understood.

"Let her go, madam, please let her go. Remember her as the beautiful angel that she was. Not as something that does not let you sleep at night."

Tears welled up in Nandita Chaudhuri's eyes and she

lowered her face and nodded her head. She looked up one last time and whispered a soft and teary eyed, "Thank you" and walked away.

"I thought you said you didn't care," I told Janardan Maity with a smile.

Janardan Maity didn't respond at once. He stared after Nandita Chaudhuri for some time, then let out a deep sigh and said, "Life can be so unfair at times, Prakash."

"I agree," I said, "how often do we see good things happening to good people?"

He seemed to be lost in his thoughts. The atmosphere had become quite heavy.

"But," I said, in an attempt to change the mood, "thanks to you, the bad guy got what he deserved."

"He had almost gotten away with it, you know?" said Janardan Maity with a smile. "I was in the blind for a long time."

"I'm curious, though. What did you mean when you told me in the backyard that I had shown you the light, and all that?"

"Ah that! Well, unknown to yourself, you had told me something very useful, and very true. You see, we always tend to respect and trust authority that comes from knowledge, don't we? As you rightly said, if I were to go to an art historian and she would tell me something about the history of art, I would believe her. Why? Because I don't know anything about the subject and she does. Her authority on the matter is supreme, and she has earned that authority through the acquiring of knowledge. Similarly, if I were to go to an expert on roses and if she would give me a bit of information on a particular variety of rose, I would believe her. Because she knows all about roses and I don't. Knowledge always leads to authority, which in turn induces trust. That was the cornerstone of Devendra Mukherjee's plan. He knew that if he were to announce that Anita was dead, everyone here would believe him, because he was a doctor."

"I see what you mean."

"And I must admit, it was those words of yours which opened my eyes and showed me the true nature of this bizarre episode. Not once did it occur to me that Anita Mukherjee wasn't dead. It was when you told me those words that for the first time, I questioned the authority of the doctor."

"Well," I smiled, "I guess I can boast of some credit to at least a part of your success in solving this puzzle then, what do you say?"

Janardan Maity looked at me with a smile and said genuinely, "More than you can imagine, my friend, more than you can imagine."

Later that night, Janardan Maity and I were having a chat, when Arun and Preeti knocked on the door to my room, and I welcomed them in.

"What a terrible mess!" Arun remarked.

"Well," said Janardan Maity looking at them in turns, "some of the loveliest flowers in the world have been known to blossom in some of the murkiest of waters."

The young couple looked at each other and blushed.

"I'm not sure what I'm going to do now," said Arun, "now that Mr. Mukherjee . . ."

Janardan Maity looked at Arun for some time. "Ashutosh Chakraborty of Park Circus is a retired Judge. He is a good friend of mine. I believe he is currently looking for a bright, honest, and enterprising secretary. If you wish, I could give him a call. I am assuming you now have some incentive to move to the city?"

Arun's face lit up, as did Preeti's. She said, "Thank you so much, Mr. Maity! You're such a sweetheart!" and having said those words, she stepped forward and pecked Janardan Maity on his cheek.

After the couple left, I turned towards Janardan Maity and smiled, "Wow! What was that?"

"I'm not quite sure," said Janardan Maity in a confused state. "I have been called a lot of things in my life, but sweetheart? No, that's a first!"

The next morning, everyone started leaving one by one. Animesh Sen came up to the veranda where I was standing, and extended his hand towards me. "No hard feelings, what do you say?"

I smiled and shook his hand warmly. "No hard feelings at all!"

"By the way," he looked behind him and stooped towards me and said in a hushed voice, "that friend of yours, he is a detective, isn't he?"

I smiled. "I'm not sure, but he himself says he is just an ordinary man."

"And you believe him?" he said with a smile.

I shrugged. "I didn't see any reason not to."

"You believe people too quickly, Mr. Ray, has anyone told you that?"

A cold shudder went down my spine as I remembered Devendra Mukherjee's calm face. I smiled wryly. "Yes, I think someone did."

He picked up his bags, and I watched him as he walked away and boarded the car that had been arranged for him.

Before I left for Kolkata, I wanted to bid adieu to Narendra.

"I was wondering if you know," I said, once I had walked into his room, "that your father had invited me here to entrust me with a responsibility, although he never got an opportunity to tell me exactly what he wanted me to do."

Narendra smiled sadly. "I think I can take a very good guess. He wanted you to speak to me. He must have felt you could convince me to come and live with him. We're cousins after all. Ties of blood."

I didn't respond. There was genuine grief in his expressions, the grief often seen on an orphan's face.

"I never wanted my father's wealth, Prakash," he shared. "I just wanted my father. But he never understood that. He was never there for me and my mother. I had won a tennis championship in school. Took the cup to his studio to show it to him, and he didn't even look at it. He yelled at me for disturbing him. He was brash and vain, and he had become an alcoholic. That's how I had seen him when we left him in Europe. When he returned to India, I hoped against hope that he would have changed. But I was wrong. He had not changed one bit; in fact he had gone farther away from me. I became more of a wretch. And after the incident with Mrs. Chaudhuri's daughter, I lost all interest in life. I tried to take my own life. It was then that he protected me, from myself. He gave up alcohol, so that he could take care of me. It was then that I discovered the father in him, and I realized that we had not stopped loving each other. But for some reason, I just couldn't tell him. I wanted to, but I couldn't. After all, it was he who had hit me that day . . . and . . . that . . . that beautiful little child . . ." He seemed to choke up.

"Narendra," I interrupted him, "you do realize that it was an accident, don't you?"

He shut his eyes. It seemed he was in a lot of pain. I realized that I had to do something. I thought for a few seconds and then said, "If you really want to repent for what you have done, then there's only one way you can do that."

He opened his eyes and looked at me.

"Clean up your life, Narendra. When Mrs. Chaudhuri said that she wanted to kill you so that your father could realize what it is like to lose a child, perhaps she didn't know that your guilt had already killed you twice over, and that your father already knew what it was like to lose a son. Think about what I told you, Narendra."

I bid him goodbye and picked up my bag, and just as I was coming out of his room, I heard him sobbing like a child.

Finally, I went to say goodbye to Janardan Maity, who stood in the study, staring towards the table at a half-finished game of chess with a sad expression on his face.

"I guess it's time to say goodbye," I almost whispered.

"Ah, you're leaving?" he said.

"Yes, and I came to say thank you."

"For what?" He seemed surprised.

"You trusted me. Without you, I would have been in trouble."

"Oh, no, I don't think so. You're an intelligent man, you'd have figured something out."

"But still, thank you, at least for believing in me."

"You're most welcome, and I do mean that. Do come to my place in Kolkata sometime. Here's my card."

I took the card and shook his hand. He put his left hand on my shoulder and said, "You're a good man. I'd be very glad to have the pleasure of your company. And remember what

I told you. You are far more capable than what you think of yourself."

***

Three months passed after that fateful weekend. I returned to Kolkata and got back to work. As is usually the case, the daily humdrum of life gradually began to erase the events of that weekend from my mind. However, there was one thing that I realized. I began to notice a certain change in myself. My attitude towards life increasingly became more and more positive. This began to show in my day-to-day activities, and in my interactions with people. I began to look for assignments more actively and my work started being appreciated. I started getting out of the house more often.

I also started working on a novel. Soon, I secured a permanent job as well. The salary was not much, but with the first month's pay cheque, I bought a new set of clothes for my servant, who had been with my father ever since I was a child. The old man wept silently for some time, raised both his hands to bless me, and went into his room without saying anything.

One day I received a small package from Narendra Mukherjee by mail. I unwrapped it to find a small ornate wooden box. Inside, there was a faded yellow piece of paper, with the following words written on it in one of the most beautiful handwritings I had ever seen -

Dear Raja,

Last night I couldn't sleep at all. But I didn't mind. He kept kicking all night, and I sat in the armchair with a hand on my belly, feeling him inside me. What a precious little thing I have inside me! Life! Indomitable, free, beautiful, precious life! Growing inside me. His nails, his hair, his skin, his tiny fingers, growing, within me. Oh Raja, I'm going to cradle him in my arms and look at him all day. I'm going to rock him to sleep and sing him a lullaby. I'm going to bathe him and dry his hair and take him out on a stroll in the garden. And in the night, when the moonlight falls on his soft skin, I will hold him up and look at his face—my moon, my star, my world, my son!

I'm sure you think of me as a silly girl, don't you? But I'm not silly, Raja, I'm excited. Oh, I am so, so excited. These are the happiest days of my life. Every night, before I go to bed, I tell my son that I love him, and although no one else here seems to understand, I feel he responds in his own little ways by saying he loves me too. One day, he will grow up to be a fine young man—honest, confident, and strong. That will be the happiest day of my life, Raja; that will be the happiest day of my life.

Suhasini

Bhaskar Chattopadhyay is an author and translator. His translations include *14: Stories That Inspired Satyajit Ray* (Harper, 2014) and his original novels include the thriller *Patang* (Hachette, 2016).

Bhaskar lives and works out of Bangalore.